Golden Handcuffs Review

Golden Handcuffs Review Publications

Seattle, Washington

Golden Handcuffs Review Publications

☆

Editor

Lou Rowan

Contributing Editors

Andrea Augé
Nancy Gaffield
Peter Hughes
Stacey Levine
Rick Moody
Toby Olson
Jerome Rothenberg
Scott Thurston
Carol Watts

LAYOUT MANAGEMENT BY PURE ENERGY PUBLISHING, SEATTLE

PUREENERGYPUB.WORDPRESS.COM

Libraries: *this is Volume II, #29.*

Information about subscriptions, donations, advertising at:
www.goldenhandcuffsreview.com

Or write to: Editor, Golden Handcuffs Review Publications
1825 NE 58th Street, Seattle, WA 98105-2440

In Memory

Joe Ashby Porter

Contents

Poetry

Translation

RESPONSE

Father

(Chapter 1 of the palimpset novel
Crime, My Destiny)

☆

Brian Marley

Did you have an imaginary friend when you were little? I did. Still do, for that matter. Name of Mr Bushell. Which by pure coincidence was also the name of the managing clerk at my father's place of business. Though calling my Mr Bushell a friend is wrong. Friendly he is not. He's the malign occupant of my right inner ear and I've tried everything short of surgery to remove him. Moreover, he's insanely jealous of my relationship with Lupin. When he deigns to make mention of her it's always in derogatory terms. *Jism-spitting whore* is one of his current favourites. I tune him out whenever I can.

Over the years he's ruined every friendship I've had, and every loving relationship too, including with Paula, causing her to stomp out and (Lupin says this is a horrible phrase) melt into the arms of another (she's probably right, she usually is). If only he'd been quicker off the mark when it came to Angela. I'll explain about Paula and Angela in subsequent chapters.

I should emphasise that my Mr Bushell was in no way similar, except in unpleasantness, to the Mr Bushell who clerked for my father. The latter Bushell was a bent scrap of a man, grey as a tombstone and obsequious to a fault. Every word he uttered sounded as though it had been buttered for ease of consumption. He never once looked directly at me, always slightly to my left or right, though I, insolent youth, stared him full in the face, hoping to provoke a reaction, preferably violent. I'd have liked nothing better than to get him sacked.

No chance.

Wizened though he was, only a fool would underestimate him. In his army days he'd chewed up and spat out much tougher nuts than me.

I suspect he thought me beneath contempt.

Father said that Bushell would become my employee when – never *if* – I took over the family business; and if not him then his son, Junior, the absolute spit of his dad, poor sod. My heart sank at the prospect. Junior was always hanging round the office, eagerly running errands and trying to outdo his father in obsequiousness. The pair of them gave me the creeps.

On one occasion I caught Junior gawping at me in the washroom mirror. He appeared to be sizing me up, though for what purpose I couldn't say. *Kill him!* hissed my Mr Bushell. *While you've got the chance. Kill him now and run for your life!* I pushed the thought to the back of my mind but didn't relinquish it entirely.

Just so you know: there was, to my knowledge, no Mrs Bushell. Perhaps she fled shortly after Junior was born or died of shame for having brought such a nasty little specimen into the world. If so, who could blame her? But no matter how hard I tried, I couldn't imagine a woman, any woman, having romantic feelings towards Mr Bushell. The best explanation I could offer for Junior's existence was that he'd been squeezed out from between his father's buttocks in a soft-shelled egg, something like a snake egg, leathery to the touch and slightly translucent.

It was hard not to feel sorry for Junior, motherless and with only his father for a suitable male role model, but somehow I managed it. I knew his schoolfellows shunned him. Friends would always be hard for him to come by, bullies an absolute doddle. His small allocation of luck had run out the moment he was born, whereas mine, already plentiful, had if anything increased. Perhaps I'd accidentally received his share. If so, I wasn't about to give it back.

~

My father is, or rather was, a well-known and highly-respected solicitor in a sleepy West Country town, and, Lupin excepted, I still have to meet a more gracious woman than my mother. But I found our comfortable middle-class existence unremittingly dull. I couldn't wait to break out of that cosy prison, to experience whatever the world had to offer a feckless charmer such as myself.

Does that sound harsh? Those who know me well know that I speak as I find, and that's what I was.

But travel would knock me into shape, I was sure of it.

To begin with, I'd wander round the crater-strewn cities of post-war Europe, then explore every last one of the three thousand islands of the Greek archipelago. Then what? Africa ...? Asia ...? There seemed no end of fascinating places that weren't situated in or near Creamer's Nook, the colloquial name for our clotted corner of Devon.

But I knew my meagre weekly allowance wouldn't get me very far, and I was vehemently opposed to the Protestant work ethic, hard physical graft in particular. I also knew my parents would disapprove of my gadding about. They had, they said, great expectations of me. My teachers thought otherwise. They were of the opinion that I was intelligent, but ... well ... lazy, if you must know. It was a word that cropped up time and again in their end-of-year reports. Lazy, lazy, lazy, lazy – one teacher after another, the bastards. Which did nothing to dent my parents' faith in me. Blind faith, admittedly, but justified in the end: I passed my exams with flying colours having done little more than flick through a textbook or two, yawning all the while and chasing butterfly thoughts.

What I studied instead, and assiduously at that, was hardboiled detective fiction and battered copies of *National Geographic*, the latter filched from the waiting room of father's business while his secretary wasn't looking.

Those were the only things I was able to concentrate on for more than a few minutes at a time.

Oxford beckoned. Or, if I fancied slumming it (relatively speaking), Cambridge. Neither appealed in the slightest.

I wondered whether I might send my Mr Bushell to one of the colleges in my stead, since obviously it was he who had done the cramming for the exams I'd taken, perhaps while I was asleep. He was, in all other respects, an infernal nuisance, and I was keen to get rid of him, even if only for one term at a time.

He'd popped into my head for no apparent reason when I was barely four years old. There I was, kneeling on a chair at the kitchen table, a simple wooden jigsaw puzzle laid out before me. The rain was pounding down and I was bored. O how I was bored. For those lucky few who know nothing of Devon, let me explain: dreary is what it is and what it's always been. The decades trickle by and nothing much happens. It rains a lot, too.

Mr Bushell's first words were *Fuck that for a lark!*

Fuck *what* ...?

'Dad,' I said 'what does *fuck that for a –*?'

I never got to finish the sentence. He drew back his hand and hit me. Hit me so hard I fell to the floor. I was, as you can imagine, stunned. This was a man who had never so much as *raised his voice* to me. I couldn't understand what had caused this sudden flash of anger. 'Don't you *ever*,' he said, each word a hammer blow, his voice choked with emotion, '*ever* say such a thing again in the presence of your mother.' Which confused me even more. Not only was mother not in the room, she wasn't even in the house. If I'd had my wits about me I might have said so, but he stalked out, slamming the door so hard the window glass rattled in the casements.

Forever after I was wary of him; reserved, polite, seemingly biddable though anything but. Whatever he stood for, I silently vowed to stand against, to loud whoops of approval (which I soon came to realise only I could hear) from my Mr Bushell. Don't get me wrong, I dearly loved my father, and I know he loved me, steadfast unto death, even after all I'd done to embarrass him – by which I mean the antisocial things he got wind of through his police contacts in the Masons. But we were never what you'd call close.

~

Those of you capable of it are probably thinking: *So this Mr Bushell, the discarnate one, the voice in his head, how could he possibly go off to university?*

The simple answer is: he couldn't, despite being of a scholarly bent. He couldn't go unless I did, and that wasn't going to happen. But there were times I felt he was trying to escape the confines of my head, to attain human form by whatever means possible. For brief moments he may even have succeeded.

It usually happened indoors, on thunderous days, when Devon was deep in gloom. As barometric pressure sharply fell I experienced a strange dragging sensation in all four limbs, as though air had assumed the consistency of water and whatever oomph I had was ebbing away. That was all the warning I got. My movements grew slower and slower until I ... I ... I ... ffffrrrozzzzze, trapped in a kind of living rigor mortis.

I soon learned to lie down before that happened and wait for the episode to pass.

Eventually, in the darkest corner of the room, I'd see a glimmer of light and a flicker of movement, barely perceptible, accompanied by an effortful grunt of the kind made by someone straining to eject a particularly hard stool; and not a shapely turd that anyone in his right mind would happily call his own, but that ugly little shit, Junior. I tried to move my head, to get a better look at what was happening, but couldn't.

Afterwards, exhausted, I slept. Then, for a waking while, my Mr Bushell held his tongue. He too must have been exhausted, and in a sulk because his escape bid had failed. He seemed to want to go every bit as much as I wanted him to leave. Neither of us got what we wanted. But I cherished those moments of peace when, perhaps for only a day or two, I had something approaching crystal clarity of mind.

Speaking of which, don't think I don't know what you're thinking. I can read you like a book. You're wondering what my Mr Bushell would have done if he'd managed to become human. Fully human, that is, like you or me, with a broad gamut of emotions and inadequacies by the score. Would he have gone off to university willy-nilly, abandoning me to my fate ...?

Of course he would! And without so much as a backward glance. No sense of loyalty, that's his trouble.

But, then again, nor had I, as you shall see.

~

It wasn't just that father had plans for me. Nothing as mundane as that. His ambitions were pharaonic. He was, of course, recognised locally as a keen amateur Egyptologist, having given a talk on mummification techniques to the ladies of the Women's Institute. He'd also donated a handful of mummified scarab beetles to the town's museum, though where he got them from I had no idea. But what also wasn't known, even by mother, was that he was the reincarnated second king of the fourth dynasty in Egypt's Old Kingdom. Khnum Khufu by name. Realization of which came to him in a dream. And that, he said, meant I was Khufu's son Redjedef, the so-called Son of Ra.

It was a view of how reincarnation worked that no-one seemed to share.

The minute mother told him she was pregnant with me, he mapped out my life from birth to death and said he'd deem it a catastrophe if mother presented him with a daughter rather than a son. He was dismissive of Egypt's queens on the grounds that, perhaps with the exception of Hatshepsut, they were frivolous and flighty. Just a feeling he had, as he readily admitted.

This he told me on my eighteenth birthday.

When his secretary went out to lunch, he ushered me into his office, locked the door, pocketed the key, took the phone off the hook so we wouldn't be disturbed and said, 'There's something you need to know'. Which, it turns out, was this:

Now that my schooling had come to an end, I would, he said, study law. No ifs or buts. And it was imperative that I avoid having to do National Service. Why waste two years on square-bashing when I could be at Oxford, studying hard and getting one step ahead of my squaddified peers? (A fellow Mason, a consultant at the Royal Devon and Exeter Hospital, could, he said, arrange an exemption on medical grounds – fallen arches, something like that.) Then, half a dozen years down the line, having secured a diamond-studded first in Jurisprudence and a gilt-edged Diploma in Legal Practice (or whatever the qualifications were; my mind was reeling and I wasn't listening attentively to what he was saying), I'd join the firm as a junior partner. Or if he was forced to take early retirement due to ill health, I'd step into his shoes – just as he'd had to do a quarter of a century earlier when grandfather became ill.

Let me explain. Grandfather started the firm in the first decade of the 20th century, and when he, Pops (aka Sneferu; though father said he thought Pops had no idea that's who he was), suffered a heart attack and had to be invalided out, father took over from him. Heart attacks run in the family, patrilineal style, and often strike while we're in our prime.

(Remarkably, the pharaohs seemed to suffer hardly at all from strokes or coronary artery disease. If they weren't stabbed or poisoned by a family member, they tended to live to a ripe old age.)

No doubt I'll have a heart attack too, though not, I hope, soon.

But that's precisely what I thought father was having when I said I wouldn't be entering the family business – not until I'd seen a bit of the world. What nowadays they call a gap year.

Most paterfamilias would, despite a thousand legitimate qualms and quibbles, support such a venture; even offer to part-finance it. Not him. He blenched, staggered round his massive teak desk and sat down hard. I think he believed he could deal with serious matters better from that stronghold than from the cosy leather chair he usually occupied. And perhaps he could. From the moment he sat in his 'seat of power' (a theatrical prop which, I suddenly realised, bore more than a passing resemblance to one of King Tut's thrones – gilt wood, carved lion heads protuberant, inlays of paste and plastic masquerading as semi-precious stones, and, painted on the inner curve of the backrest in the symbolic, two-dimensional style of that distant epoch, a group portrait of himself, mother and me) my resolve began to fade.

'Charles,' he said, clutching at his chest, both of us aware that a stressful situation such as this could induce a fatal heart attack, 'please say you don't mean it.'

O but I did, though I didn't want to say so, not again; I knew it would only make matters worse. A change of subject was urgently needed. Better still, if I could manage to slip away without making it look obvious ...

But of course the door was locked.

'Dad, you look awful peaky. Shall I fetch a glass of water? Hand me the key and I'll –'

He shook his head and glanced towards the filing cabinet

which, as everyone who was anyone in our little town knew, was actually a well-stocked drinks cabinet. He raised three fingers horizontally and I poured the requested measure, adding a bit extra for luck. His favourite tipple: Lagavulin, an Islay single malt. The glass was full almost to the brim.

'Ah,' he said, 'that's the spirit I like to see.' Unsurprisingly, given the circumstances and the marked quaver in his voice, the joke fell flat. He took the glass from me two-handed, to stop the whisky from spilling, and gulped it down.

As the colour flooded back into his cheeks he relaxed a bit and so did I.

'Look, Charles,' he said, his voice a little firmer, 'I realise that what I've told you will have come as a shock. As pharaoh, Redjedef was a disappointment, one of life's notable underachievers. He ruled for just eight years, which is probably why, according to the historical record, his sole accomplishment was a half-built pyramid. But that really shouldn't be held against him. Pyramids take decades to plan and construct. Because of the need for secret inner chambers and labyrinthine passageways, some with no purpose other than to thwart future generations of grave robbers, they're complex structures, much more so than their plain exterior would suggest. They're also resource heavy and extremely labour intensive. An additional factor is that the pharaohs, viziers, high priests and nobles, together with officials of lesser rank, such as architects, quantity surveyors, project managers and slavemasters, were blundering along, doing their best to learn from previous mistakes and in the process making new ones.

'But mistakes on such an epic scale inevitably cost lives. Even during the construction of *half* a pyramid the death toll must have been enormous. Their legacy is – I apologise for using such a melodramatic phrase, but there's no better way of putting it – steeped in blood.

'You'll do better than that, Charles. I know you will. According to the cardiologist your heart is sound, so time is on your side. Assuming you get off to a flying start. And deep in your subconscious you'll have learned from Redjedef's many mistakes. If you dive into that vast reservoir of knowledge, things will go swimmingly.'

If only I could. My inner Redjedef has yet to be found. Had

I the habitual suspicions and gut feelings of some of the brighter sparks in the Met (few in number, I'm glad to say, or I'd be writing this from behind bars), I'd suspect my Mr Bushell of doing away with him. Unless, of course, my Mr Bushell *is* Redjedef.

Lupin, an expert in narrative poetics, says speculation of that kind leads nowhere. Moreover, it slows things down: 'Like trying to run a mile in lead boots'.

Point taken.

'Dad,' I said, 'you're right about not wasting valuable time. Of course you are. And believe me, I'm keen to become a solicitor, just like you.'

O how the lies trip off the tongue.

'Foreign travel can easily be postponed, but National Service cannot. When my call-up papers come, I must go. To do otherwise would be morally indefensible. I couldn't live with myself if I tried to wriggle out of it. I mean, I know it's important to get my career off to, as you just put it, a flying start –'

'And jet rather than turboprop, Charles. A Boeing 720, maximum cruising speed 611mph, rather than a Handley Page H.P.7 Herald 200, which has, I'm sure you recall, a top speed of only 272mph, even with the benefit of a stiff tailwind.'

Father the plane buff, flexing his knowledge. Aviation being an interest we'd once had in common.

What he didn't know was that I'd long since grown out of it.

Every little secret I kept from him broke a link in the chain that bound us together.

Also, I have to say, I found his regurgitation of irrelevant facts at inappropriate moments deeply embarrassing. No surprise there, then; adolescents find almost everything embarrassing.

But I spared him my blushes and he said, 'Time is pressing, my boy, therefore speed is of the essence.'

'I agree, Dad. Wholeheartedly. I want to be a solicitor more than anything in this world. More than life itself. But surely queen and country must come first. Defence of the realm tops higher education. So wouldn't it be better if I wait until I come out of the forces and then see how I feel? Not, I hasten to add, that I'll feel any different to how I feel now – that's impossible. A solicitor I was born to be! A pharaoh, too, I suppose. But you've acknowledged that the time you spent in uniform did you a power of good. This is what you said:

To my surprise I didn't mind the drill, exercises and bull. Remember that?' (No reason why he should. I was winging it, making the whole thing up as I went along, desperately hoping I wouldn't hit a bum note and even if I did his tin ear wouldn't detect it.) 'What's more: *The army stiffened the sinews, encouraged self-discipline and gave my life purpose and meaning.* That's what you said and it's precisely what I need. It's also where you met Mr Bushell, isn't it? *Catterick's top drill instructor bar none,* you said, *capable of striking fear into the hearts of new conscripts by the simple expedient of never raising his voice above a sinister purr.'*

'Did I really say that?'

'Which bit?'

'About him being the top drill instructor?'

'You did.'

'Really?'

'Last Christmas. You were in high spirits and may have had a tot or two over the limit.'

'That explains it then.'

'Explains what?'

'Why I can't remember saying it. Any of it. I'm not even sure the drill instructor bit is true.'

'Ask mother, I'm sure she'll remember.'

I knew he wouldn't. She disapproves of his drinking, which is why he does it mostly during office hours, one tot at a time, in the gap between appointments.

To be honest, I'd hoped that by mentioning Mr Bushell I might soft soap him into accepting my argument – a strong argument, even without the Bushell factor. But he glanced at his watch and his eyebrows shot up.

'I can't deal with this right now, Charles. Terribly sorry. I'm late for an appointment with Mr Lovegate about –'

I raised a forefinger, stopping him dead in his tracks. 'Let me guess, Dad. Might it be – just a stab in the dark, as they say – some kind of boundary dispute?'

He gave a snorty laugh and whisky fumes wafted over me. 'As ever. You know this business almost as well as I do, Charles, which is music to my ears. Lovegate is incorrigible. Now that the neighbour to the north of his property has had a stroke and is in a persistent vegetative state, Lovegate vs Claypool cannot proceed.

Certainly not in the short term. Probably never. So he's keen to tackle his neighbour to the south.

'There's also the problem of a well-established public right of way to the rear of his property. Not only has he fenced it off, he's topped the fence with barbed wire and, according to a seriously injured rambler, set a bear trap, the kind once used in parts of North America to catch grizzlies. Photographs of the injuries to the rambler's leg would make even a reconstructive surgeon wince. Only yesterday a trap, possibly the same one, saw-toothed and bloody, was retrieved from a shed on Lovegate's property, so it's extremely likely he'll face criminal charges, to which, no matter what advice I offer, he'll plead not guilty and be found guilty. Meanwhile, in civil court, he's suing the rambler for trespass, with no greater chance of success.

'Not that he'll see it that way. He's an angry, bitter, thoroughly unreasonable man with deep pockets and spendthrift ways. Since, against his expressed wishes, his wife Peggy died of cancer (it's common knowledge that she did it just to spite him), he's become increasingly litigious. It's an obsession. A monomania. His every waking hour is spent tilting against windmills and trying to right imaginary wrongs. They probably fill his dreamlife, too. And even though he's invariably the one in the wrong, we try to represent him to the best of our ability because, it goes without saying, what's best for him is best for us. You wouldn't believe how much his chippy disputatiousness swells the company coffers.

'But look, Charles, much more importantly, we need to decide what's best for you, and there's no time to do that now. Please be at home at six o'clock and we'll have a proper chat about it.'

Best for you? Hah! Best for him, more like! growled my Mr Bushell. *Typical pharaonic bullshit! He must think you're a total fucking imbecile. Which of course you are – goes without saying – I've been telling you that for donkey's years, fat lot of good it's done –*

Etc., etc.

He really does go on.

~

I'd like to be able to say that the verbal sparring between dad and
me ran past the chimes at midnight and into Sinatra's wee small
hours of the morning, the timeless time when exhaustion sets in,
eyelids droop, and planet Earth stops spinning ... or seems to. That's
when my cast iron logic and superior oratorical skills (so powerful
in combination that even Demosthenes, perhaps the greatest orator
of all time, would have been impressed) caused dad to fold his
metaphorical tent and steal up the little wooden hill to ... come on,
you know where: the county sandwiched between Cambridgeshire
and Buckinghamshire, its larger and more affluent neighbours.

'O for crying out loud, Charles! Stop being such a bloody
awful show-off!'

'Can't be helped, Lupin, my love. It's in the genes. Redjedef's
genes, I suppose. A foible. Beyond all measure of control. So be
patient my hypercritical angel, my editorial but never dictatorial
poppet of poppets, be patient and –'

'Charles, I'm warning you!'

'– hear me out –'

'Charles! Stop! Not another word!'

'– and enlightenment shall be yours, because, sad to say,
that's not what happened. Quite the opposite, in fact. When push
came to shove my eloquence fled, taking my argument with it. The
'proper chat' lasted barely ten minutes: dad exeunt triumphant.'

'*Charles!*'

~

It was horrible.

And on my birthday, too.

I was devastated. But I wasn't going to have my life plans
thwarted so easily.

The following morning I took a bus to the army recruitment
office in Plymouth and signed on for the duration: four years and
three months. Poor old dad. Because I was one day over the age of
consent, all he could do was put his head in his hands and groan.

It was a ploy, of course – on my part, not his. The army
wasn't for me, nor me for it. Being shouted at while marching up and

down. Shouted out of our cribs at some ungodly hour of the morning: 'Hands off cocks, pull on socks', etc. Shouted at while at chow or in the latrine attempting a chow-fuelled bowel movement. Army life seemed to consist of nothing but parade drill and route marches in the rain, up hill and down dale, accompanied every waking moment by shouting.

(Despite its effectiveness, Bushell's sinister purr hadn't caught on. Nor would it, given that it was a figment of my imagination.

Lupin: 'This is irrelevant, Charles. Totally irrelevant. I'll edit it out later.'

'Even though my imagined reality is often stronger and more compelling than actual reality?'

'Even so.')

Driven to distraction, I took to stuffing pellets of bread in my ears, to deaden the sound.

The only useful thing I learned in the army was how to handle weapons; guns in particular. It would pay off handsomely in years to come, though I didn't know it at the time.

But what I did know was that, after a grace period of twenty-eight days, I could give the army two-week's notice and return to Civvy Street, free to do whatever I fancied.

Which is precisely what I did.

A mere six weeks after leaving Devon under typically thick cloud cover, I was happily ensconced in Soho, outside a pub, in thin winter sunshine, supping a pint of London Pride and minding my own business.

Then along came Billy.

Meditations

☆

Susan M. Schultz

MEDITATION 11

1/10/20

It's a story they tell themselves that makes sense of their lives, he says. A story links race to rape, rape to the military, thus to America's wars of imperialism and back to rapes, to orphans. Then throw adoption in. Take the walkers away from sex offenders, someone writes, so they can't provoke our pity. They can walk after they're declared not guilty, can't they? He had a good experience in the Boy Scouts, but his abuser had been a scout leader. He had an abuser who was a scout, but his grandfather was a kind man. Variables sing out from flawed equations, demanding restitution. There's need for a Rage Park where we can pause to scream, throw bones to ourselves and chase them, unleash ourselves in a controlled space. The problem with containing rage is that it resists the container, spills through netting or chain link that holds it in. An arm across the chest signals love and confinement. The wedding photo showed his arm around her neck. The murder dressed as suicides came later. Someone left the abuser to die in his cell and threw out the video evidence. It means denial can masquerade as hope. It's not just trauma we push down, mistaking silence for safety. It's also positive emotions that go into hiding in the city's sewers or basements, those things with feathers avoiding the street, angling for cultural amnesia. A schoolyard fills with terrified kangaroos, fleeing the bush fires. Bet you hadn't expected that migration. Texas will take no more refugees, as they've done their share. Who parcels out these shares, or keeps the graphs of their rise and fall? Who has victimized whom? Do not look at yourself in the mirror. I posted the photograph of a dead saffron finch on instagram; it lay belly up on the sidewalk beside the culvert, its neck so bright a yellow it appeared orange, with fragile orange beak. Does memory preserve or desecrate the bird, whose photograph I take and post on instagram? It garners lots of likes. Is it the beauty of the dead bird's plumage, or the framing of bright color by gray sidewalk? Decomposition composed. Camera as stun gun, fired at whatever you least want to change. Or can least resuscitate. My daughter finds it odd that I take pictures of dead birds; she saw a dead mouse, but refused. The Tibetan monks who meditate beside a charnel pit are not so shy. To see oneself as flesh, then bone, then dust, makes our being's imminent absence visible. Immanence is no lie, though the stories the President tells are yarns. He took photos of homeless persons' blankets, so as not to invade their privacy. She holds up the brightly colored quilt she made for her son. The last ever, she swears. Make sure your conclusion is less an ending than an opening, and leave off the moral of every story told.

MEDITATION 12

1/14/20

I am just a peg to hang his cursive meditations on. When I ask my students to offer up a quirk, one says he's an English major who doesn't read. He used to read half a book before he put it down, but now he doesn't get even that far. Very few in our generation read much, says my daughter's friend, the one who's reading Thich Nat Hanh on dying. At night they turn on *Baywatch* for the bodies, not the plot. But bodies *are* the plot, machines to make prompts for our writing exercises, the ones our parents worry about because we can't make money off them. She realized quickly that thinking might help her earn money, so she went to class. I argue for inherent value, but that's as quaint as poetry itself. Do nothing for ten minutes a day, I put on my syllabi; if this seems too hard to fit in, remember it's a course requirement. If I could give credit, I would, but the value inheres in practice and practice makes good enough. Somewhere in the middle of that question, statement took over, the rhetorical hammered into bronze, like a statue that walked out to sea at the end of a novel I've forgotten. If earning is like memory, accruing value over time, then forgetting takes us back to living within our meaning. A small bird sits outside my window on the brown rhapis palm frond, but when I look back from my writing, it's gone. We await the dropping of the next shoe. It's hard to fight corruption, because it's spongy, and it gives and gives before folding into itself, feeding the next salted wave of paranoia. It's formalism, really, but without irony; the more you work at the poem's structure, the less you find between the ribs. I explain my dog's name by citing the woman who didn't require a man's rib. Hard power defeats soft every time, with occasional exceptions for martyred saints. Her personality is extremely rare, as she puts connections over division, others above herself. Another student comes from a family of six kids and two parents, all of them vegan. Sitting beside her is the woman who likes the all-you-can-eat meat bar. It's a diverse society, but you have to be taught to express yourself. He governed his tongue in class because the toxic TA policed everyone's words. We want everyone to be better, so we demand specific sentences of them. A man on the radio said (this was the late 60s) he thought "brainwashing" was when you took someone's brain out of their body and gave it a bath. For our next class, consider why we write while Australia burns.

MEDITATION 15

1/20/20

The world ends in hail and dust. No more a consistent tense that moves from present to present, but a tense confabulation. It's a powerful move, I tell my students, but you need to know where you're going. It's not that we're all living in the present, rather that its fragile shell so easily shatters. Memory loses all category, as if the past only rewound the present. My mother confused my story with hers, my husband with hers. Who's to say we were not all on that plain, huge orange dust storms sweeping toward us, enveloping our drone-witness, bearing material prophecy in its grit. The dust cloud is 186 miles long and moves at 66 miles per hour; it crests over Dubbo and Broken Hill, composed of earth from farms in New South Wales. "Look at the earth," my father would say, meaning the orange clay that only broke when you took your spade to it. The earth was that color in Vietnam, a vet once told me. But now it rises as if it had wings and its poet wasn't always so stoned he heard angels singing, their verbs blooming dutifully at the ends of sentences, where they propel us back to the beginning, no matter their tense. Our witnesses watch for us, a drone hovering over Diamond Head to see how many houses burned on the first clear day in weeks. It was such a beautiful day. Without my uttering the word, my students talk about mindfulness, this being in the present, being with, not coming after. Legions of bearded white men descend on Richmond with their guns; one chides a younger man for using the word "masturbation." We're here to show our love for each other, he says, and the younger man avers, backing off. One wears a knitted American flag hat, the other an orange bandanna. Love does not alter where it alteration finds, is bronzed like another horseman in another instagram photo. Yesterday, I saw Ronald Reagan on a horse, as still as a church mouse. The drone came back to the park like a boomerang, though after the third news story it's running in the present, coming back and back to spill its video record. She read out loud from *To the Finland Station*, sentences unspooling like Krapp's tapes, students giggling at their heft. At the Atocha Station, I thought I saw old women selling bats on sticks, suspicious that the poem was an act of realism, not experiment. There was a plaque for the intervening dead. Some species may be rendered extinct by the bush-fires. To be going extinct. What tense is that? The continuous perishing.

MEDITATION 16

1/21/20

She says the neighbor was sitting on his truck bed while his daughter played on the swings yesterday. Today, he told me he was close to both of the dead officers. Marcus Aurelius writes that we observe everything before we're 40. From then on, it's a loop. We get used to things; we put a distance between us and our injuries; we reconcile ourselves. We forgive the trespasses of those who trespass against us. (Wisdom literature leans forward and back.) Aurelius would recognize the absurdity of this weekend's violence: an old man killed cops with a shotgun, then set his neighborhood on fire. If reality presses against our eyelids, then how can we close our eyes? We keep them open to our devices, real and imagined. Distraction may have gotten us here, but it had better save us now. An Englishman once asked me why Americans use "gotten" instead of "got" as a verb form. I assured him we do not. Two sentences later, I heard myself say "gotten." How little do we know ourselves by our verb forms. They make a fine family tree, however, enough to launch a holy book. Had he gotten help, he might not have run amok, the angry Czech. I want a how-to on looking, while not suffering for it. If I make my sentences longer, they might lose their hurt before the period waves its penalty flag. Can I offer wisdom before the facts, like a trial set up to occur before any witnesses are called? It's a rough path, life, my son writes, though his photograph is of a wall. No matter the angle, the edges are blunt and sharp, and each fork in the road gets you there. The president has done nothing wrong, his counsel says, so there's no need to introduce evidence. We're watching the death of democracy on our screens, but it's not entertaining enough, so we'll do it quickly. No wonder our tenses are inconsistent. What occurred before the trial must be presented after the trial is done. Acquit him first, then argue that the evidence comes in too late. There's a crisis in comedy, but I haven't watched any for years now. The transcript of an absurdity is like a garden tool used to injure your landlord. "Kill da landlord," Eddie Murphy screamed. It was funny then, but it isn't the day after the landlord cannot be found dead in her own home, burned to the ground by her tenant. You can't tell the joke, if the punch-line comes first. Or the shotgun blast. She let him stay in the house because she took pity on him.

MEDITATION 17

1/24/2020

The man with the blank map keeps calling you into his office. The
man with the blank map in his office points to blank portraits on
the wall. We see that they were men, but they are featureless. All
that's left of their histories shows in gilded frames, cleansed of dirt,
that glint beneath the ceiling lights. The blank map man screams
profanities, but the next day he will attack you for your "lack of
decency." The blank faced men in frames cannot look out or in. A
senator refers to himself as "visibly upset"; perhaps he has a selfie
to prove it, because neither in nor out will do what at requires. Look
within thyself and write, or look at thyself and whine. A good portrait
keeps his eyes on you as you cross the room. The eye that sees you
is more powerful than a weapon, because it gives you pause to think.
"People will hear about this," said the man with the map, intending
it as a threat. What is most dangerous is someone else's attention
to us. I will sit quietly in my office. I will not say to anyone what they
might repeat to another. My mask is a map with nothing on it. I know
it covers a place, but I cannot stick a pin in that place. The memory
police are out to shame us, but shame has no currency. None of
my students ever drew the face of a quarter with any accuracy. We
cannot see what we use. A gumball means more than a founding
father. Chew on that.

MEDITATION 18

1/26/20

I hadn't seen him in a while, the gray-haired white man who walks
the one-eyed dog named Rosie, sometimes yells at traffic to stop.
He'd yelled at me, too, about Hillary, about lazy millennials, about the
university, about how people just don't look out for each other any
more, about people who drive through stop signs. A radical centrist,

he called himself. For months after, I talked about his dog and mine, the weather, anything neutral (weather over climate, I'm sure). The last time we'd met, just past the new year, he'd yelled at me about "rag heads," and I called him a racist. Turned on my heel. Today, as I came up Hui Kelu with Lilith, I saw him and Rosie ahead of us. He saw us. At his turn-around point, he crossed the road, started back toward his townhouse on the next street over. He had sunglasses on, wrap-arounds. I said, "good morning!" but he kept going. His body clenched tight: arms out from his sides, legs moving like pegs. The only softness to him might be his belly. He's my lesson, but it's a lesson I cannot learn. Perhaps he's happy in his horrible opinions, a friend opines, but I don't believe it. He's how pain turns to Fascism; he's how hurt accumulates grudges; he's how you come to hate a woman neighbor who wears an Obama shirt, so clearly a "snowflake," even in paradise. He's how you don't avoid your pain, but alchemize it into anger. It's more valuable that way. He's how you take someone aside, abuse her, and then call her indecent. He's how the mirror works. The man who yells at traffic sees me on his mirror, but not as myself. This confuses me, like the times my demented mother transposed herself with me. So accustomed to seeing myself in the mirror, I saw the image of someone I didn't want to know.

MEDITATION 19

1/30/2020

On the Friday the Republic dies, there will be a sale on our words. They're more valuable to us as empty containers than as pith. The store that sells us on organizing will stack them at the windows, inviting us to use "democracy" to store our beans, "due process" to hold our rough drafts. My students find the sonnets uninteresting, incomprehensible. Yes, there's a speaker in the poems, and yes, he's hectoring a friend. He wants his friend to "breed." He wants his friend to last forever, as a collection of words. But we'll sell those, too, like the banana taped to a wall that sold for $250,000 before someone walked up and ate it. The banana gives us mental energy; I may be remembering my former students' names because I ate one this morning. It's useful, and to suggest otherwise is a joke. An expensive one. They shake their heads at the thought. Is it a joke on intrinsic value, on art's rot, on the usefulness of duct tape, or do we take it at its word: "banana"? I'd tape mine to a wall if I could, then take your good money to dispatch it. If I no longer own the word "idealism," I cannot be disappointed when it proves useful in a service economy. The word "hoard" explains a lot; so does the border wall that falls in a stiff wind. One field has to do with economies of love, the other its sickness. The best words aren't just empty; they're translucent in the way plastic is, admitting light while blocking clarity. The former dive instructor said there were days she surfaced into fields of plastic. I urged her to start there, that's an Image we can hold onto. Beneath the ground-cover this morning, I saw a yellow toy smile at me. I took its picture.

MEDITATION 20

2/2/20

She knew a woman who lived in the house of the woman who died at the hand of her tenant, by fire or by gunshot. The woman who owned the house worked in the library; she looked familiar. She belly-danced. I might have seen her at the old Egyptian place, a middle-aged white woman thrusting her belly forward, my friend's partner's straying eye but brief. Anne was guardian ad litem at a house where a sumo wrestler was killed over meth. Next door, a young mother beat her son when his kind step-dad was away. Up the hill, a man keeps his disabled parents hostage on the lower floor, while he goes surfing in his van. We tell ourselves it's always been bad. That despair is their friend, not ours. The practice is about facing death, but we think of that death as ours, not our republic's by which it stands, one nation indivisible, with. The poems aren't so much about love but the damage we leave, if we're lucky. He wants to translate old poems into new, render them honest in their confessions to inadequate feeling. I open the old poet's book and find an inscription to me,--"with love," two days after a birthday. He gave me a bear hug in a thick sweater. Lived in an old fire house with his poet's wife and children. Paid ambivalent homage to Stevens, though he was a Williams man. This is what it will be like,

Bryant says, putting one foot in front of the other, not calling attention
to yourself, not saying what might be reported. Cloak your words,
as in a poem. (And take his name out next time.) The reader comes
later, but there will be no trace of you at your place of work. Soon
to be acquitted, the president rescinds the ban on landmines. Just
because he's guilty doesn't mean we should convict him.

Toy Town

☆

John Muckle

Jack Mudie felt he was a shadowy figure to his family, obscure even to himself. He put down his phone and sat quietly at the desk in his bedroom. The bamboo blind was down but sunlight filtered through its slats, lending a little warmth to his dusty living space. His papers were strewn about the floor, teaching materials mostly, unpaid final demands for council tax, water rates, and what have you. But what exactly did he have? A view, for one thing: a room with a classic view, if he cared to look out at the trees and what have you, the da-da-da, and opposite the lit windows of other living spaces.

The blossom and the leaves had come quickly this year, as if squeezing themselves violently into existence following a long period of turbulent weather: unseasonable snow, icy winds, bursts of tropical heat. What was going on in the eco-system of the world as they had known it? Frankly, he didn't care all that much. In between scuttling forth on his journeys across the city, Jack had spent the past few months assembling memories, fancies, and splurges of invention into something he was calling, to himself, a novel, although in some quarters there might be disagreement about this appellation.

As his fingers flew over the keyboard of his laptop or scribbled out his inspirations in notebooks, he'd been wondering how he had the cheek to call what he was doing invention, imagination, storytelling, or any of the other fudgy terms for composition, narration, scribbling, and moulding into unity. Theirs had been in his estimation a whatever period in human history, and in his own life as he spiralled on towards his final years. Perhaps this was it, and that was that.

His mother was dying in hospital, not at home as she would have wished, and his father was refusing to visit her. No amount of bullying or cajoling by Mikey, his brother, was going to make any difference to that. Jack had sat quietly beside his mother's hospital bed, spooned ice cream into her dry, sunken mouth, and tried to make out words in the faint mumbling sounds which sometimes came out of her mouth. Dad was in bits. He'd sat with his father, listened to his brother hammering on and on. Sometimes he thought the sole purpose of his brother's rivers of speech was to batter him into submission, bang nails into his head, and to prove for the last time Mikey's superiority and dominance in the family, his greater worthiness of the name son. All this 'man-up' shit. Telling his poor stricken father to 'man-up'. Fuck that. His need for authority. Basically, he was a pain in the arse, they both were.

Jack wanted to abandon him, once and for all to leave them all behind, his clinging family with their tedious repeating loops. But he spent a lot of time alone, and his own repeating loops were not much more beguiling. Is that all human beings were made of? A few strips of worn out tape spooling around the brain's playback heads forever, a few tones that beat out 'me, me, me, me' forever, until the game was up? People were pushy, more or less so, but few were truly reflective. This went for Jack Mudie himself. Wasn't it possible that what he passed off as hard-won wisdom was merely the recurrence of opinions and attitudes he had arrived at sometime near the get-go of his conscious life, or before, and that he now ground out fresh-minted as points of final destination? More than possible!

One thing his writing had taught him was to be aware of how little he himself knew about anything – things he was supposed to know, for instance, like his supposed nearest and dearest (though he could make a stab at them, he felt), and beyond this a whole murky world of relationships, systems, and ideas that others seemed to dance through with such confident aplomb. But he could only sketch them in vaguely, in accordance with some ideas he'd inherited from somewhere or other – and it was always the worst ones which stuck firmest, occluding earwax muffling the world, leaving him with vague sonic guesses that invariably turned out to be wrong.

When you were wrong it was like being locked out, losing your key, or even worse being supplied with a replacement key that didn't work. This had happened to Jack very recently. He'd dropped his keys he knew not where. After ringing his downstairs neighbour's bell, he got into the flat by removing the cardboard he'd put up and reaching through the window he'd broken with a large stone last time he'd lost his keys, a wire-reinforced pane which he hadn't bothered repairing because he knew it would sooner or later happen again.

At the Housing Trust, there had been a bit of an argument. A rather stern, moralizing woman whom he had never seen before but who seemed now to be in charge, informed him that his request to borrow the master front door key to the house was out of order, just not possible. His downstairs neighbour had told him that the keys were impossible to copy anyway, she having tried twice to have hers duplicated for her son, who had stayed with her for six months a few years ago.. Jack duly told her story to the woman at the Housing Trust, which seemed to have changed her mind, if only to contradict him and his ill-informed neighbour. What she had been lacking in was this woman's permission to cut a key.

Meanwhile, the younger woman, pretty, mixed-race, well-dressed, who sat at the front desk, smiled wryly and said it wasn't a problem. She fetched the key (which he had to promise the older woman he would bring back before five o'clock) and took the master over to their designated locksmith ("Extortionate!" said the younger woman) by an unfamiliar bus they helpfully suggested to him.

These were smaller buses than the usual kind, and the journey he made to the locksmith (a journey which was to become familiar) followed a long and winding route through hilly North London streets. It was a beautiful journey, the small bus half-full of women and young children, friendly, chattier than they would have been on a full-sized bus, and the dark orange houses were residences he would have loved to have owned. Who had originally lived in them? What class of people, and what had their lives been like? These were questions he had often asked himself but had always been unable to answer satisfactorily. This didn't prevent them from popping up again.

When he reached the locksmith's, the man behind the counter took the passkey from him, found a blank and fitted it to his cutting machine. He popped the correct holes and grooves into it mechanically, without removing his mobile phone from his cheek. Jack paid fifteen pounds by card and was shortly handed both master and a duplicate along with a receipt. He enjoyed the return journey on the half-size bus more than he had his outward trip. This time a small boy had waved at the driver, standing with his mother and sister at the side of the road and waving until they were out of sight. Jack had waved back shyly.

However, once back at his home address, he discovered without real surprise that the new key didn't work – although the master did, perfectly – and he wondered if perhaps the downstairs neighbour hadn't been right: somehow the keys were actually uncopiable. She had also remarked that Turks were untrustworthy; they would say anything. Jack wondered if there might be something to this, although the man at the locksmiths, the locksmith, in fact, had not been Turkish.

Nevertheless, he made an immediate return journey on the miniature hail-and-ride vehicle that pushed through the same sloping avenues of attractive villas, again admiring the filigreed decorative flourishes in the brickwork of some of them, their overwhelming design-grace, as always preferring those with the original window-fittings. This time another man was also riding on the bus, pricing a minor building job on his mobile. Jack could not tell exactly what it entailed, nor did he particularly care – but he heard the man pointing out that he and his partner had been doing similar work for years, suggesting politely that his prospective customer could phone around for more quotations and, if he was still interested, get back to him. Middle-aged and dressed in working clothes, the man got down at the next stop, leaving Jack to his anxieties.

He was worried that – five o'clock fast approaching – the locksmiths would be closed by the time he got there. But when he did arrive the key-cutter was no longer speaking on his phone, and he carefully compared the master and duplicate keys before refitting them to his cutting machine.

"Sorry about that," he said after a couple of minutes, casually handing them over. "Should work now."

"What was the problem?" Jack asked.

"The first cut wasn't deep enough."

"The first cut is the deepest, hmm?"

"Now it is perfect," said the locksmith.

He trudged back to the bus stop outside Sainsbury's to pick up the return bus to where he normally resided. While he was waiting there for it, a small man with long dreadlocks sprinted past them across the carpark, his arms full of clothes on hangers he had evidently stolen. The thief kept glancing behind him, without slowing his pace, but he wasn't being chased. All the people at the bus stop turned to watch him pass out onto a further road and make his escape.

This time a young West Indian woman boarded mid-way through the journey. Wearing a pair of loose men's trousers, struggling on crutches but with a radiant face, she addressed the other passengers.

"Is it just me or has it got a lot colder today?"

Several of them agreed vigorously, shivering, turning up the collars of their coats.

"It's freezing!" she exclaimed, smiling at all and sundry, obviously feeling that she was giving voice to some closely-guarded secret, speaking of something about which they had as usual been misled by the authorities.

She found the weather mysterious. So did Jack. Would they wake up in the morning to golf-ball-sized hailstones? He remained sceptical about the key until he pushed it into the lock and found that, this time, it did indeed work to perfection. But he was too late now to return the passkey to the Housing Trust. It would have to wait until the following morning, he decided he would drop it off there on his way to work. The downstairs neighbour had remained behind her own locked door, unavailable for further questioning about the misinformation she'd blatantly proffered earlier on.

Keys were indeed a difficult business, and once you had one available you would be wise to keep it close at hand, if not firmly within your grasp, at all times. He kept his in his left trouser pocket and felt the top of it with his thumb frequently. A few days later he ran downstairs in a hurry to fulfil an obligation in Chingford, only to find he was locked in: in a further mysterious twist, the front door lock had jammed. The neighbour spoke at length, as usual, then phoned the Housing Trust whilst he sat on the stairs to wait. Within the hour, as promised, a representative of the designated locksmith had arrived to repair the defective mechanism, but Jack had already called Hazel Miles to cancel his tutorial session with an overlong explanation.

Travelling back and forth between the town he lived in and the rural place where his parents and his brother resided, Jack had begun to notice a strange but interrelated series of phenomena. It was as though the reality of one place was partly obliterated by his being in the other. When he was in his parents' bungalow he found the details of his urban life and the places it took place in started to become vague generalities about the places and people in question, and when he was at home the reality of their place, his parents' place, darkened like a map withdrawn from torchlight.

The effect was certainly one of darkening and lighting up, but being in the lit-up place obscured the details, almost blotted out entirely the place that had fallen into shadow. As if the existence of one precluded the other, although there was no proper relationship apart from the long thread of railway track running between them. Therefore, to think or speak of one place whilst in another was difficult, to say the least, and certainly different than speaking or thinking of the place you were actually in.

But then, he realized, this was no more than a subjective phenomenon, amounting only to an experience of how little real detail he retained, how quickly it decayed and floated away, how little he solidly knew about either place or the people who lived in them. Out of sight, out of mind. The mind, his anyway, really was feeble when you got right down to it, although powerful as well since it was able to generate a whole cartoon version of imaginary places to replace them in their absence. How completely the reality of other people dropped way when they were gone, leaving only shadow puppets in a theatre of his somewhat lacking imaginings.

It was a disappointing insight into himself, for all that it was one that he (and others?) had gone on living with for quite some time. It was a matter of picking up and putting down, stepping into a set of half-familiar relationships, or trying to hop from one place to the other. An act of mental reconstruction was taking place every time, he realized, an effort which produced poor, softened, self-serving reflections of those people and places he was trying to bring to mind in his recollections, putting them in order as he went, giving them a final so-called 'life' in his so-called novel.

All his became particularly obvious and painful when it was his own particular mother dying in her generic hospital bed. She was slipping away forever without ever having been known, or so it seemed, and conversely it became difficult for Jack Mudie to believe that he himself had ever – except perhaps in childhood – been anything more to her than a dimly apprehended shadow, a glitch in her mind, an irritating shadow moreover which frequently angered her by not behaving as it should in her own puppet theatre version of the world, as they had watched it slowly disintegrate under the onslaught of her growing dementia. But he knew, they all knew, that she had always been mad, and furthermore he believed that they had been the main cause of her insanity.

Anyway, this is perhaps why the towns he dwelt in remained strange to him, and why he remained an outsider in them both. Running through the strange town, surviving due to inefficiencies in the administration, the lack of mesh and cohesion to be found in their hollow notions of community and representation. Did he believe in any of this ridiculous crap? How might it have turned out for the best?

In the winter, his father used to take the gearbox off a car and carry it upstairs to their council flat to work on in front of the fire. Newspapers were spread on the carpet, and a sheet held over the fireplace to get the flue roaring, until it finally caught alight and flew up the chimney, and all those words flew up with it, glowing for an instant then grey flakes drifting away: that was their world, it had gone forever, and good riddance to its facsimiles, thought Jack.

Fitting cogs together, scrubbing wire brushes in petrol baths, worn bushes all carefully replaced, reassembled, all to make ends meet. Except they didn't always, they sometimes flapped loosely in unrealized, unsingable songs, and at the end of a week he and his mother scoured the flat, looking down the back of the red settee for pennies: worn or not, twelve of them would buy five Players Navy Cut, and he'd been sent down to Iris, in the middle shop, to hand them over. He'd felt no shame in this. On payday, a comic he'd eyed for many weeks would at last be his: Classics Illustrated, *The Black Tulip*. It was a rare flower, coveted by all who saw or heard of it, grown in a greenhouse in old Amsterdam by careful selective breeding.

One snowy Christmas day he'd unwrapped his first guitar. How its tan sunburst had shone! He'd started to strum on it tonelessly, slowly learning to play Silent Night and Old Black Joe. Gone are my friends, from the cotton fields away. Keith Steel, a merchant seaman, lived in an upstairs flat with his mother. Here and now, in the strange town, Jack remembered him in his sailor suit. He'd given Jack an old guitar of his own, a slightly better instrument, darker anyway, with ancient varnish that scraped away in powder under his fingernail. Keith's guitar had a battered air of having accompanied a drunken merchant seaman over the seven seas.

He'd tried to learn 45s, destroying them one by one on a wind-up gramophone. Jack needed lessons. His mother suggested he should ask Mr. Hopkins, from the last shop, the grocers. A lucky guess. Behind his white coat, cheese wire, whirling bacon slicer, and a jar of broken biscuits on the counter, he was a retired amateur jazz musician with a grey goatee who played guitar and soprano sax. He'd taught Jack on Fridays, early evenings. Chords, simple classical pieces. Jack's fingers had been too small for the fretboard, Mr. Hopkins' wife always knitting an endless cardigan, and towards the end of the lesson she would bring in unbroken biscuits on a plate, coffee in small green cups. Once, after much persuasion, Mr. Hopkins had taken out the treasured Soprano and played them his tune. They'd sipped and listened, listened and sipped. Ain't Misbehavin'. Mrs Hopkins glinted behind her winged spectacles, knitting, because he was savin' all his love for her.

If you really wanted to be a drug dealer in London, not just a fake one like Gay Tony, your best option, the best job you could possibly have would be as a bus driver on one of those winding hail-and-ride routes. They could just put their hands up with a couple of twenty-pound notes in their palm, and the driver would stop and pull a wrap out from behind his counter. The mayor could issue you with a special licence to carry a weapon. Nah, said Maleek. That's clever, but you would soon be caught. They got cameras all over them buses. Not the little ones. Hmmm. Tyrone a no show. Sally put him in the sitting room to wait. Again, it was an experience of being locked in. She'd removed the inside handle. It was her punishment room, Tayone said after he'd turned up and been debriefed about his mock exam performance.

Jack hadn't minded being Sally's prisoner. A beautiful, sexy woman whose harsh tongue inflamed his Wednesday evening sessions with an (as always) half-reluctant boy, she had put in only the briefest of appearances, just enough, more than enough, to make her a ft. She looked like Kelly Rowland, Queen of Nellyville. Did she think of him when she was with her boo? Jack purposely spun out each and every conversation past its tolerable limit: a few seconds before she slammed the front door in his face.

When he went down to be at his mother's bedside, he had noticed Mikey's head was shaped like an unopened bulb, bulging but tapering away at the top; a sprig of hair remaining on its summit formed the wisp of a question mark above his large eyes. They were sitting in the Highfield Social Club. The place was half-dead. *Don't Look Back in Anger* played on the jukebox, put on by the clutch of twenty-somethings clustered at the end of the bar; to them a classic of twenty years ago, it reminded Jack of the woozy, unhappy hedonism of the daft university students he'd been teaching at the time. It put him in a place he didn't mind remembering.

The barmaid sent over a couple of glasses of something that tasted a bit like anisette. Brought to them by a thin, youthful woman from the Midlands. She had four grown-up children and had been one of their mother's main carers. Maybe it had been her idea. She was a lovely woman. At last Little Richard came on and Mike told him something he'd recently read on Wikipedia about his career. Jack felt at a wrenching distance from it all, as perhaps did Mikey, but no, he had been playing tapes as usual.

Peace to him, peace to all of them. After all, they hadn't asked to be related to him any more than Tyrone or Maleek had demanded he give them English tuition. The former polite and thoughtful, although completely uninterested, the latter bouncing off the walls of Hackney Youth Hub. One of the naughty boys, as his mother had described them to all her carers, with one of the last of her smiles, her face alive with irony.

Earlier on, his brother had shown him the latest of his dioramas, constructed of model cars and accessories he'd bought over the internet or had found in Taunton. It was a scene from the late forties of a woman standing beside a silver Airstream caravan, looking obliquely out with her arm raised to shade her eyes towards

what might be a horizon. Her husband, in knee-length shorts,
prepared to throw a frisbee for a jumping, excited dog. Behind him
was a Nash Countryman of the correct year and a downloaded
wraparound photo of the landscape of the Rocky Mountains, below
them a piece of Astroturf cut to fit the top shelf of one of his car
cabinets. The other held his reconstruction of a Studebaker garage,
with two Golden Hawks in different states of repair, one of them
undergoing restoration on a ramp. Mikey had got him to try out his
virtual car racing set up in the spare bedroom, and also performed a
couple of magic tricks.

They sat and drank until closing time, and as usual Jack felt
his brother's slight irritation when he turned down his tilted-glass
offer of one last drink. He'd had enough, enough so that he felt a bit
unsteady as he tottered around to their parents' bungalow. His father
was still listening to the radio in bed, which struck him as a good
sign of something. Jack had fallen asleep straight away in relief, as
he usually did after one of these long, strained sessions.

Now he was back in town at his desk in front of the sticky
keyboard at which he wrote his dirty little books. Jack Mudie. The
man without a story. But there was a wisp and a wire curled up
around here somewhere, a final connection always to be made,
at which point the whole gizmo would light up like Christmas and
begin to whirr a little bit. The windmill on the music box would turn
again. The Antelope would leap from its signboard and become a
real antelope, running like hell to get away from the two White Lions.
And so it would all come out straight and true in the end. Suddenly,
through the fog of this belief, he remembered the absolute certainty
with which his father once demonstrated the action of a magnet
upon iron filings, the unerring patterns they made, the invisible
field of astonishing forces, and the important idea – held to have a
mysterious explanatory power – that like repels like and opposites
attract; leaving him to pry the two magnets apart for himself with his
small, grappling fingers.

Dad remembered, those special moments that seemed to
define something for him. Do you remember when we worked on
that Buick? Comes out of nowhere with that smile, and Mum used to
curate these moments of his sometimes, mentioning them, imbuing
them with further portent and significance. The lord had spoken.
And it wasn't even that she particularly revered his defining memory

moments herself, although he 'often mentioned' them, just that she thought that he, Jack, should mark them, remember them, guard their meaning. Do you remember when we worked on that Buick? As if that was the only moment of contact they had ever achieved, was it really the only significance his eldest son's entire life had for him?

It wasn't, of course, but there was always something irresistible to him about the way these things fell out, offering themselves up for meaning like the wishbones of Christmas turkeys they had eaten long ago in his childhood, prised apart between his father's short blunt finger and his own pink twig. But who would get tho biggor half, who would be allowed to make their silent wish?

Making somebody else listen to your memories was like showing off your gold filling. A way of registering your contempt for them, with a none-too-appetizing treat. If you are noticed at all it is as a denied influence at first, doomed anyway to become memory's tool in one way or another; automatic cheerleader to their inner theatre of recollection, internalized approver of dubious exploits still at a planning stage. For every Saturday afternoon sports watching armchair ham there was a mum on hand with an ever-replenishing round of ham sandwiches. Without her dark energy to drive them, they would all flop down, like broken puppets.

Dad, always with a smile on his face at the thought of a car, a bike, lighting up in company like an extension-lamp plugged into the grid, the grid. Jack had always admired him for having a job he liked, being a mechanic, which he might deny, but it was the whole of the best part of him, finally what had made him be like himself.. Not so chirpy nowadays, devastated by mum's death, he held *Motorcycle News* in his mottled brown hands, he read all day long, not trying to reconnect, watching the rebuilds on the rebuild channel, rubbing away at the hours until he himself was rubbed out.

All these ridiculous things were prodded towards you, and fatefully, faithfully, you picked them up. His father had always got the main part of the wishbone, and it had turned out just the same this time. The lion's share of suffering was perhaps his final prize. It had been more than he could possibly bear, yet somehow or other he had done so. He appeared unchanged, the only way they could really accept him. And at the end of the last day, he was alive to watch cars being rebuilt on telly and read the motorcycling papers. Mikey brought them around for him, kept him talking.

Stationers Park was a long narrow piece of ground which tumbled down between two nearby streets, amongst the most agreeable in all Toyland, red and stately, suitable for Christmas cards, framed by a procession of alien pollarded trees on the steep hill from the top on which Jack had recently taken a photo with his phone, only to be asked by a passing woman if he happened to be David Icke, or 'Ick' as she pronounced it. Finally, the penny had dropped with him, who she was referring to, but fearing she might be a follower of his instead simply said that no, he wasn't the lizard-fancying conspiracy theorist. "But you are him," she had insisted. "You look exactly like him." Jack had apologized for not being so and descended the hill to his assignment in the beautiful Christmas card house, actually a well-appointed foster home, a surly runaway of a boy who was determined not to be inspired by anything, not even stories about space and long multiplication.

Jack was back there today, wandering around the park, biding his time, drinking an Americano at a trestle table before his weekly torment with the lad. It really was a pretty little park, locked up at night, a river of brightly dressed children continually streaming around it from top to bottom, either in school uniform (he had once seen his tutee hiding under his jacket passing through), or gambolling at the side of responsible-looking young middle-class parents wearing whatever they had now instead of kagouls, carrying those modest frayed bags stuffed with anything sensible a child could possibly need, their awkward, slightly frail looking bodies obviously bursting with inquisitiveness and intelligence. The park had everything – a dried up rocky stream with a muddy pool at the bottom end, a stony bridge you had to clamber across, holding on, a couple of tennis courts, the back end of a mid-Victorian church now repurposed into fifteen flats, the vicarage still next door, and at the top of the park a trio of bowl-like baseball and football courts in which a few boys wearing sharp sports strip practiced in the early summer evening. A few groups of mums and adolescents sat around smoking and chatting at folded steel municipal picnic tables.

Something about the place, its continual ambulatory circular traffic, reminded Jack of the cliff top garden at Sidmouth where he and his brother had scattered his mother's ashes, partly at a bench looking out to sea, partly beside some shrubs planted in a clump around a secluded bower. Both had a certain holiday gaiety he supposed, something worn-in and reflective, public memory gardens with open lockable gates. She would have liked the park, Jack thought, as he tried somehow to mentally attach her to it, but she would not have wanted to stay long or come back. It was a pleasant place, lovely enough, but mainly for young people not old ones like herself and Jack. He would do just as well to avoid it himself in future, and probably would not be returning often to the Sidmouth cliff garden either, much as mum had loved its fragrant borders, its mini-amphitheatre, its old potting sheds and greenhouses for bringing on cacti. Maybe there was something about places where you scattered ashes. You didn't really want to go back to them. You had a kind of secret with those places – not a public memory. Mr. Jinx flowed down from the shoulder of her ruby dress, a river of tortoiseshell fur.

My Oulipo Year:
On Editing
The Penguin Book of Oulipo

☆

Philip Terry

In February 2018 I received an email from Simon Winder at Penguin Books asking me if I'd be interested in curatiing an anthology on the Oulipo group. This sounded too good to be true, and immediately I suspected a wind-up. The clue was in the name, surely: Winder. "What should I do?" I asked one of my closest friends, Liz Vasiliou. "Just say ys," she replied, with a nod to Perec's e-less novel *La Disparition*. So I did. Simon Winder, it turned out, was a refreshingly enlightened senior editor at Penguin, and a distinguished writer himself, who shared my enthusiasm for French literature – we were both fans of Patrick Modiano and Henri Michaux – and who was involved with many of the projects which have recently reinvigorated the Penguin list, such as the new Penguin Freud. We met up in his office in the Strand, in an imposing building which reminded me of some of the fascist architecture I'd seen in Lyon the previous year, and after a brief chat he asked me to draft a proposal. The proposal I put forward, and which was quickly accepted, was for an anthology which not only consisted of writings by the members of Oulipo, the staple fare of such an enterprise, but also included important precursors, what Oulipo call, not without a sense of humour, their "anticipatory plagiarists", as well as a representative samplng of the growing number of exciting writers outside Oulipo who have blazed the same trail. A book of three parts, in a word: Before Oulipo, Oulipo, and After Oulipo. Putting together an anthology of Oulipian work in English was something I'd already been thinking about for some years, but it was the kind of slow-burning project I thought I'd probably bring to fruition in my retirement. Now I had to do it in a little over eight months.

For the last twelve years I'd taught two courses on Oulipo at the University of Essex, and I'd corresponded with and met many Oulipians over the years my first novel, *The Book of Bachelors*, each chapter of which was a lipogram in a different letter, I'd sent to their President, Paul Fournel, in 1998, and he had written back enthusiastically – so I wasn't exactly starting from scratch, but at once I set about reading everything I'd neglected to read in the past. I read the 80 fascicles of the Bibliothèque Oulipienne (limited edition pamphlets published by Oulipo exploring their latest ideas) which I had ordered for the Albert Sloman library at the University of Essex library a couple of years back, but never got round to reading; I read all the French novels and poems of the one English member of Oulipo, Ian Monk, only to come to the conclusion that they were too difficult to translate successfully, steeped as they were in French argot; I read the playfully political novels of Oulipian Jacques Jouet, though found that the extracts I would need to represent them with any justice were far too long for the number of pages at my disposal; I spent a week at the Oulipo Archives, the Fonds Oulipo, in the Biliothèque de l'Arsenal in Paris; I visited the Queneau Archive at the Biblithèque Armand Salacrou, in Le Havre; and I read Lauren Elkin and Scott Esposito's *The End of Oulipo?* (2013), where they argue that Oulipo has run its course, dissolving into the creative quagmire of "Oulipo lite", though to my mind their arguments, based as they were on the existing English language translations of Oulipo alone, and neglecting poetry entirely, were wide of the mark.

And as time was pressing I did something I'd usually shy away from, that is I met up with and talked to influential people in the field to pick their brains. I met David Bellos, Perec's principal translator, who happened to be in London to record a radio feature on Victor Hugo, and he at once suggested a number of chapters from Perec's *Life A User's Manual* for inclusion, as well as a little-known aleatory music score by Perec from the 1970s, "Memory of a Trip to Thouars". I met Alastair Brotchie, who had edited *The Oulipo Compendium* with Harry Mathews, in his office above the Bookartbookshop in Shoreditch, to quiz him about the connection between Oulipo and 'Pataphysics; when I mentioned the *Dossier 17* of the Collège de 'Pataphysique, where the first collective publication of the Oulipo had appeared in 1961, he leant backwards and pulled it off a nearby shelf. And he alluded to the Journal of the London Institute of 'Pataphysics, which had recently published some music scores by members of Oulipo's spin-off the Oumupo (or Workshop of Potential Music), by the likes of Gavin Bryars. And I met the American poet Lee Ann Brown, who was on a residency in Cambridge, to discuss some of the American poets and writers who had written Oulipian works, and the often overlooked connection between Oulipo and the New York School, and beyond this to the Language poets, like Lyn Hejinian and Charles Bernstein, who had also experimented with constraint-based writing.

Over the previous year I'd been fortunate enough to be included in the Expanded Translation network, organised by the poets Zoë Skoulding and Jeff Hilson, and by a happy coincidence the network included a fair number of Oulipophiles. Lee Ann Brown was one of them, whose own magnificent work often works with Oulipo, and who Harry Mathews had invited to contribute to *The Oulipo Compendium*. In the end Lee Ann hadn't taken up the suggestion, she had felt she was too young at the time, but she was thrilled at the prospect of being included in the Penguin anthology, and was generous in sharing her extensive knowledge relating to the dissemination of Oulipian ideas across the US poetry community, which culminated in the noulipo conference at the California Institute of the Arts in 2005. This had been set up to explore Anglophone responses to Oulipo, often of a deliberately politicised persuasion, on the surface a hundred miles from Oulipo itself, which had deliberately avoided political affiliations, after the disastrous consequences of Surrealism's flirtation with the Communist Party. The network also included the poet Lily Robert-Foley, a founder member of Outranspo (the Workshop of Potential Translation), which had been set up to explore Oulipian methods of literary translation, the poet and translator Cole Swensen, who had translated many Oulipian texts, some of which she generously offered for the anthology, including a translation of Michelle Grangaud's *Poets' Calendar*, and the poet and critic Vincent Broqua who pointed me in the direction of Jacques Roubaud's novelistic memoir *Peut-être ou La Nuit de dimanche* (2018), which had caused something of a storm in Paris for its apparent critique of Oulipo, largely relating to what Roubaud percieved to be a corporatisation of the group, moving away from the concentration on invention, recommended by co-founder Raymond Queneau, to a concern with the history of the group and its public profile.

I took advantage of my contacts in the UK poetry scene, too, asking for suggestions from Tim Atkins, James Davies, Holly Pester and Peter Manson, among a host of others, and soon I was deluged with material. I'd planned, ambitiously, to include 100 pieces, but before I knew it I had in excess of 200, and the problem quickly shifted from what to include to what I had to leave out. Among the magnificent pieces I had to drop for want of space was a brilliant piece by Tim Atkins, who had written a novel called *The Bath-Tub*, then rewritten the whole thing using Oulipo's N+7 method, where nouns are substituted by moving seven places forwards in the dictionary. Then last but not least, I took up an invite from Oulipo, which I'd been ignoring for a couple of years, to come to one of their monthly meetings as an *invité d'honneur*. Thinking about this now, I can't remember why I'd been putting this off – perhaps a combination of shyness and an unwillingness to actually meet in person these Oulipians that I had come to revere so much, just as when in the 1980s I'd spotted Samuel Beckett drinking in the *Petit Café* I avoided going in to speak to him, just sat down on a nearby bench, lit a cigarette, and thought: "That's Sam fucking Beckett!" But then again, it perhaps had something to do with my own writing too. While much of my writing has been enabled by my engagement with Oulipo – *The Book of Bachelors* is a case in point – I was also wary of this becoming an overriding influence, and some of the work I'd written that I most cherished was not really Oulipian at all. I remember sending my version of Dante's *Inferno*, relocated to present-day Essex, to Harry Mathews in 2014 – he said it wasn't remotely Oulipian, even if it leant on his translation method "up-to-date", but called it "a smasheroo".

Eventually, just as the 2018 World Cup was coming to a close, an event which had been a constant companion during my reading binge – and surely it was a good omen that the French team were hitting their stride again – Simon Winder came to visit me in Wivenhoe, where, after a brief tour of the village, including a peek through the window of the house where Francis Bacon had briefly had his studio in the 1950s, we went through the material I'd gathered together. We agreed on 100 pieces, and discussed ways they might be organised. Simon mentioned the idea of a sort of "rattle-bag", perhaps with Heaney and Hughes's poetry anthology in mind, where the reader is free to dip in and out as they please. I mentioned the possibility of organising the pieces according to the method Perec uses in *Life A User's Manual*, where the order of the 100 chapters is determined by the knight's move in the game of chess. It took three weeks to actually work this out, and in the end the results were disappointing. I was reminded of the passage in *Life A User's Manual* where Perec describes how the painter Hutting devises an elaborate formula for his portraits, where colour is dictated by the date and time of the painting's "birth" and the phase of the moon at the painting's "conception": "The system's impersonality," Perec writes, "was the kind of thing to captivate Hutting. But perhaps because he applied it too rigidly, he obtained results more disconcerting than captivating." So I tore it up and started from scratch, working with that most un-Oulipian resource, instinct, trying to stitch together an order that would actually work as a reading experience. I hung on to the idea of Perec's non-linear organisaton, however, interleaving works by Oulipo with anticipatory wordsmiths and fellow travellers, and worked by way of repetition, contrast, groupings, and juxtaposition, as one might in a novel. A sequence of Oulipian memoirs (short autobiographical texts beginning with the phrase "I remember..."), predating and post-dating Perec's own *I Remember* of 1978, and beginning with New York artist Joe Brainard's 1970 book of the same title, would be dispersed throughout the book in order of composition (I included memories 1-20 from Brainard, 21-40 from Perec, and so on); the chronological order of the before and after Oulipo would be disrupted, so that Homer, say, one of Oulipo's precursors (like Homer, Oulipo love lists), could be juxtaposed directly with the texts that it linked to most clearly; sequences of sestinas, or

explorations of the acrostic from Perec and *The Psalms*, would
be presented side by side, a move that became possible once I
decided to label each piece with titles like "Oulipo", "Anticipatory
Plagiarism", "Noulipo" and "After Oulipo". In a similar manner Theiri
Foulc's "New Observations of Harry Mathews's Face", where he
distorts a portrait of the writer's face by reference to the letters in
his name (A=1, B=2 etc.) was juxtaposed with Rabelais' *Gargantua
and Pantagruel*, where scale is similarly played with, to suggest a
continuity of interests across the centuries. Even if every reader
wasn't going to pick up on all of these subliminal links, just as in
the first reading of a novel some aspects of the work's architecture
escape us, it gave the organisaton an inner cohesion, which I hoped
would come across to readers as a general feeling that they were
in good hands. And if strict chronology was disrupted here, then
that seemed fitting to Oulipo. For one thing, some seminal Oulipian
works, such as Queneau's *Exercises in Style*, first published
in 1947, actually predated the founding of Oulipo, while some
"anticipatory plagiarists", on the other hand, such as Joe Brainard,
whose *I Remember* first saw the light of day in 1970, came after
Oulipo strictly speaking. If Oulipo in some ways works outside
conventional time, I had a first hand experience of this in connection
to 'Pataphysics. After meeting Alastair Brotchie, I talked to him
about visiting the Pataphysical Museum in north London, where a
large archive of Oulipian work was held. It was late August 2018, so
when he said why not come along to the Pataphysical New Year, I
initially thought that was quite a wait. 'Pataphysics, though, I should
have guessed, follows its own calendar, and the New Year falls on
the 8 September, in the month of Absolu, marking Alfred Jarry's
birthday. All was well. Perhaps one day somebody will set up the
Outempo (the Workshop of Potential Time) and bring some order to
bear on Oulipian concepts of time. Meanwhile we will just have to
muddle on.

One Oulipian strategy which I did stick to was to organise the
introduction alphabetically, after the manner of Kevin Jackson's
alphabetical essays, which worked well, and came out feeling
natural, and it helped keep a rhythm in the introduction, stopping it
from getting too long and boring – I've never been a fan of overly
long introductions, and have a tendency to want to skip them and

get on to the the actual text itself. Similarly, I didn't want an excess of footnotes – these were supplied only where the introduction didn't have the space to introduce an individual piece, or where the sense would otherwise remain obscure. I wanted to give enough information so that the reader could make sense of what was before them, but after that to leave them alone to read. And yet, while my initial plan, following an anthology edited by the then President of Oulipo, Paul Fournel, the *Anthologie de l'Oulipo* (2009), was to create an anthology where the reader was presented with a series of texts which read well in their own right, rather than create the more common anthology of constraints, I didn't want to disappoint the reader interested in constraints either – so I included an index of constraints where these could be pursued by the curious. This seemed fitting, as there is an argument in Oulipo as to whether or not constraints should be revealed, and this method enabled them to be revealed, but at the same time partly concealed by not presenting them up front, as it were. And it also paid homage to Oulipo's love of indexing.

Two things I drafted but didn't include in the end were dates with individual pieces and notes on contributors. There are many key dates in the introduction, but including dates with each individual piece was problemmatic. For one thing dates are often multiple with Oulipo – Queneau's *Exercises in Style* was first published in 1947, though many of the pieces date from much earlier, and a number of the pieces included here date from Queneau's revised edition of 1973, where he removed several pieces he thought inadequate and included a series of new ones which consciusly Oulipianised the book (pieces which are not included in any previous English translation). Gilbert Adair's translation of a passage from Perec's *La Disparition* (1969) is another case in point. Here, Adair substitutes Poe's poem "The Raven" for Baudelaire's "Les chats" ("The Cats"). Not only does his translation tip into pure invention here, but in giving us this text by Poe, he slyly introduces another of Oulipo's anticipatory plagiarists – Poe's essay "The Philosophy of Composition" (1846), where he discusses the mechanics behind "The Raven", has long been a key text for Oulipo. As often happens with Oulipo, this combines to make dates problemmatic, so that they cannot be given in the straightforward way favoured by historians. Perec's novel dates from 1969, but the passage from 1994, or, more correctly, perhaps, to January 29 1845, the date of the first publication of Poe's poem in the *New York Evening Mirror*. Where notes on contributors are concerned I ground to a halt when it came to Homer. It's all very well giving a thumbnail sketch of a contemporary author – so and so is the author of such and such – but with Homer this seemed inappropriate, and the idea started to unravel. I thought that I could probably assume that my readers would *know* that Homer was the author of the *Iliad* and the *Odyssey*, they might even know that "Homer" was possibly even an invention that had been attached to the products of an oral tradition, so for me to concoct some kind of bio-note started to seem ridiculous: "Homer, though not to be confused with the character in *The Simpsons*, may well have been a family man, we don't know for sure, but scenes of domesticity abound in his two most distinguished works...."

I'd stick by these editorial decisions, even if some of them were necessarily made on the hoof, but they were, perhaps inevitably, found annoying by the odd reviewer. The historically minded couldn't understand the ordering, and wanted an ordering by date of composition, and others wanted author notes, and mistook the fact that there wasn't a note for *every* text as an indication that I had somehow not finished the notes, complaining that the editing here was lazy. Another, who came from my home town of Belfast, drove the point home by pointing to misspellings in the text. I couldn't help thinking at this point that Belfast must still be under the yoke of the spelling test, as it had been when I was a child, as it remains under the yoke of the British government. The misspellings, though – such as "an" for "and" in Harry Mathews's *Trial Impressions* (1977), to give only one example – are actually part of the Oulipian texts themselves, and are common in Oulipo. Perec's novel *Les Revenentes* of 1972, where the only vowel employed is "e", is full of them, and couldn't have been completed otherwise. And Raymond Queneau, the co-founder of Oulipo is famous for his phonetic spellings, as in the opening of *Zazie dans le métro*: "Doukipudonktan?" ("D'où qu'ils puent donc tant?" or "How come they stink so much?") Misspelling takes us to the very heart of Oulipo, in fact. Lucretius's *De Rerum Natura* (*The*

Poem on Nature) supplied Oulipo with one of its key concepts in the "clinamen", Lucretius's Latin for the Greek *klesis*, "a bending". The term was rescued from obscurity by Alfred Jarry, who used it for the name of his Painting Machine in his novel *Life and Opinions of Dr. Faustroll, Pataphysician*. For Oulipo, it represents a moment when a particular constraint is broken, usually for aesthetic reasons – but it is something which should only be used when it is also possible to complete the writing task without breaking the constraint, and it is something which should be used sparingly. In Perec's *Life A User's Manual* each chapter desribes one of the visible spaces in a building with 100 such spaces, but the novel contains only 99 chapters. Perec's missing chapter is the clinamen. For Lucretius, the term has a specific sense, referring to the spontaneous deviation that allows atoms falling in otherwise parallel lines through the void to collide with one another and thus create matter. Without the clinamen, in other words, there is no creation. Elsewhere in his argument, Lucretius likens atoms and letters, arguing that just as small changes in atomic structure can alter the nature of matter, so small changes in words can alter sense, as in the words "fir" and "fire". All of a sudden, Lucretius's description of the creation of matter starts to sound uncannily like a description of Oulipian wordplay, and from this perspective clinamen can be seen to describe not just creative deviation from a rule, but the creative swerve involved in any textual manipulation, such as the N+7 method or homophonic translation, or, indeed, *misspelling*.

And perhaps there is a similar philosophical point to be made concerning our contemporary desire for author notes, as if the identity, tastes and biography of an author were all that were needed to explain the literary text. It was Roland Barthes in his essay "The Death of the Author" (1967) who did most to popularise the idea that the concept of the author was essentially a Romantic notion which functioned to close off meaning in the text, and who argued, by way of contrast, that a text could be seen rather as a tissue of quotations from literature, culture, and history, the author as no more than a performer in a tradition that always already exceed the self – and perhaps it is for this reason that Fournel in his *Anthologie de l'Oulipo*, edited with Marcel Bénabou, includes no names next to texts, just the author's initials, as if to suggest that Oulipo as a collective endeavour is more important than any individual author? Oulipo themselves were very aware of both structuralism and post-structuralism, movements with which they had much in common – the minutes to their monthly meetings, held at the Bibliothèque de l'Arsenal in the Fonds Oulipo, reveal that they had plans to invite Roland Barthes to one of their monthly meetings, though the plan never came to fruition, and Italo Calvino's novel *If on a winter's night a traveller* (1979) uses Barthes' essay as a template for its exploration of the reader in the text, where the reader becomes an active producer of meaning. Calvino's novel, on one lovol, io a creative embodiment of Barthes' Ideas In action, and the same could be said of other Oulipian texts vis-à-vis structuralism. In Oulipo, the point raised by Barthes' essay about *who is writing* is nowhere made more clearly than in Perec's essay "Think/Classify". Here Perec meditates on Oulipian Marcel Bénabou's "One Aphorism Can Hide Another", where Bénabou creates a machine for the production of aphorisms. In brief, Bénabou dissects aphorisms into their underlying formulas, such as "X is the continuation of Y by other means", then creates lists of word pairs, such as false synonyms (love and friendship), and antonyms (science and ignorance). By combining these formulas systematically with the lists of word pairs, he is able to generate an almost limitless supply of new aphorisms. Perec concludes: "Where is the *thinking* here? In the formula? In the vocabulary? In the operation that marries them?"

Once I submitted the manuscript for *The Penguin Book of Oulipo* there were other hurdles ahead. The manuscript itself was more like a collection of photocopies than a traditional book manuscript, and there was a lot of work still to do to make it into a book, and then there were unforeseen problems obtaining rights which at moments threatened to derail the whole project, and which were only ironed out by a frantic summer of letter writing, telephoning, emailing, and meetings – one of these a lunch at which I was presented with a pork chop having forgotten to mention I was a vegetarian – with the people managing the estates of Georges Perec, Stefan Themerson and Stanley Chapman, to name but a few. My meeting with the members of Oulipo, though, went smoothly. I was reassured by the relaxed gathering at the home of Ian Monk, round plentiful bowls of curry and rice, where what you didn't want to eat could easily be dodged, and where the agenda was written out on the back of an envleope, and proceedings were as affable as they were chaotic. There was little sign of the corporatisation that Jacques Roubaud had complained of, and there was no sign of a diminution in the Oulipo's enthusiasm for sharing and exploring new ideas: Olivier Salon discussed at some length Oulipian ideas, such as palindromic formulae, that he had recently unearthed in French science fiction novels; Pablo Martín Sánchez presented poems written on a cylinder, whose meanings changed as parts of the cylinder were rotated; Daniel Levin Becker presented poems that explored the constraints and patternings of English bell-ringing scores. And as I told them the story of my own engagement with Oulipo, which began in 1977 when I came across Calvino's *The Castle of Crossed Destinies*, and was cemented when, working as a lecteur at the Université de Caen in the late 1980s, I came across the Gallimard paperback *Oulipo: La Littérature potentielle* in Fnac in my lunch hour, all listened attentively, butting in from time to time and sparking off heated discussions at every other word.

One late editorial decision had an impact on how I think about the book now, and led to a few late adjustments. Right up until the last minute the notes had been at the bottom of the pages, and were fairly restrained, only added where sense would otherwise be opaque. The introduction was there to give a broad context to Oulipian writing, and to many of the individual pieces, too, equipping the reader to make sense of pieces themselves. Yet a late move of the notes from the bottom of the page to end-notes seemed to remove the need for brevity so that a sense of a lack was created – if one piece had a footnote, why not another? It was never my intention to supply a note for every piece – some are explained in the introduction, as I have said, some are self-explanatory – but for the satisfaction of future readers a few additional footnotes will be supplied for the paperback, sometimes pointing to the idea behind a particular juxtaposition, such as that with Rabelais and Foulc. Apologies to future readers if occasionally this strategy errs on the side of telling rather than showing – but remember, you can always do what I often do, and ignore the notes.

3 Poems

☆

Roberta Olson

Finite Differences

It all happened so quickly
Instead of being rounded by a sleep
We are rounded Into integers
I prefer daydreams to psychology
If you raise the blinds a little
It almost sounds like music
In the click and hum of appliances
Where everything is automated
We know to walk along a certain street
With a mix of magic, comfort and longing
We circle the buildings
Speaking in birdsong
The night is habitat and
There is a sad irony
In the three note song
Of early morning birds.

Notes of Unseen Birds

I start running, finally I am back
The last warm day of the year
A soft white haze and the scent of rain
I woke up to find my eyes
Glued together
The room was painted white
And did not belong to me
I wanted my vision to be
Something fierce and hungry
Like a hawk, an eagle, a cat
But the dark blue doors were locked
Certainly someone upstairs
As the rain pours
Grey day, grey feathers
Something got a bird
It is best not to rub your eyes

Totem

The second day is the hardest
Tuesday morning small bird outside
I was nothing but an enormous eye
In a universe of sound
The loud flat slap of rain
The soft thud of pillows
Falling on the bed
Dark lace of music
Tinny through the walls
What shapes to make a tower of sound?
The bicycle wheel and the shadow it cast
The shadow of a lily made of lead
Without a totem the story
Spins out of control
Your physical presence in the world
Elusive as a pirouette

Two sonnets by Paul Valéry

☆

translated by Ian Brinton and Michael Grant

I
Au Bois Dormant

La princesse, dans un palais de rose pure,
Sous les murmures, sous la mobile ombre dort,
Et de corail ébauche une parole obscure
Quand les oiseaux perdus mordent ses bagues d'or.

Elle n'écoute ni les gouttes, dans leurs chutes,
Tinter d'un siècle vide au lointain le trésor,
Ni, sur la forêt vague, un vent fondu de flûtes
Déchirer la rumeur d'une phrase de cor.

Laisse, longue, l'écho rendormir la diane,
Ô toujours plus égale à la molle liane
Qui se balance et bat tes yeux ensevelis.

Si proche de ta joue et si lente la rose
Ne va pas dissiper ce délice de plis
Secrètement sensible au rayon qui s'y pose.

(first published in *la Conque*, November 1891)

I
Sleeping Beauty

The princess lies asleep inside the palace of briar rose
Beneath the murmurs and the moving shadow;
And unclear words are mouthed in coral
As lost birds peck at her rings of gold.

She listens neither to the falling drops
That chime with beauties of a wide and distant past,
Nor to the fluted breeze in shimmering woods
That tears in two the clamour of the horn.

Let protracted echoes lull the dawn reveille,
You are always more than equal to the sinuous creeper
That dangles down and taps against your shrouded eyes.

Moving so slowly and so close against your cheek
The rose will not dispel these tanglings of dolight,
Secretly aware of sunlight resting there.

II
Le Bois Amical

Dédié à André Gide

Nous avons pensé de choses pures
Côte à côte, le long des chemins,
Nous nous sommes tenus par les mains
Sans dire…parmi les fleurs obscures;

Nous marchions comme des fiancés
Seuls, dans la nuit verte des prairies;
Nous partagions ce fruit de féeries
La lune amicale aux insensés

Et puis, nous sommes morts sur la mousse,
Très loin, tout seuls parmi l'ombre douce
De ce bois intime et murmurant;

Et là-haut, dans la lumière immense,
Nous nous sommes trouvés en pleurant
Ô mon cher comagnon de silence!

(first published in *la Conque*, 1892)

II
Friendship's Wood

Our minds turning to the purity of things
We found ourselves side by side
Holding hands in silence
On the path…among dark flowers.

As though betrothed we kept in step
Through meadows of green night;
Tasting of unimagined fruit together
Beneath the moon, good friend to the demented.

After which we lay there on the moss, unmoving,
Distant and alone beneath soft shadows
Of the intimate and murmuring wood;

And above, in an immensity of light,
We found ourselves again, both weeping –
Firm companions of the silence!

2 Stories

☆

Curtis White

The Terrorist is a Suicide Bomber #1

For a hundred years or more the world, our world, has been dying. And not one man, in these last hundred years or so, has been crazy enough to put a bomb up the asshole of creation and set it off. —Henry Miller, Tropic of Cancer

He didn't look Middle Eastern. Perhaps you could say that he shaded toward Mexican-American with a trench coat and a soul patch. To my eye, he looked like a Gen-X gone pachuco. You'd half expect him to pull an iPad out of a snazzy leather shoulder satchel, either that or hop into a low-rider, chrome hubcaps whirling. But you'd never pick him out of a police lineup as the guy you saw running down the street with a rocket launcher on his shoulder.

I've never really understood the hatred he seemed to inspire in most places. In rural areas, simple folk would see him and strap Colts to their waists, daring him to come forward—as if he'd bother to harm any of those jokers. He had nothing to add to their misery. For him to kill someone carrying a gun in one hand, a bag of Doritos in the other, that was not his style, and they were not his concern.

And what was his style, you might want to know? Good question. I once put it to him and he replied, coyly, "My spirit ricochets in tiny windows."

Oddly, in most matters unrelated to his *metier*, the Terrorist was a "people person," as those Dorito munchers would have known had they given him just a little of their idiot time. Those who did give him the time were surprised to learn that he was a terrorist. "He seemed so nice," they'd say to the news cameras. As for me, I always felt good around him, and I must be the furthest thing from a terrorist—a writer of books, if you will.

Painfully, he had no one to share his goals in life with except me, and that was only because I wanted to write a book about a "homegrown" terrorist, a sleeper cell of one, something that the *New York Times* would run as a series of investigative reports, a book with a six-figure advance to follow. So, I was always eager to listen to whatever it was he had to say. If this seems selfish and exploitive to you, it's probably because it is selfish and exploitive. But that's a writer's trade. There's no substitute for it.

The interesting thing—and this is something the morally gelded *Times* certainly won't be interested in (although the mangy book industry might)—the interesting thing is how often I abandoned the role of neutral observer, how often I was recruited to his purposes, how close I came to his mode of belief, in short, how eagerly I "went native." But that is something that you'll be able to see for yourself as my story unfolds. It's not particularly subtle. You may judge me as harshly as you like, but for the moment I ask for an open mind where the Terrorist is concerned. I ask for your "willing suspension of disbelief" that a terrorist can be sympathetic. I even ask for your compassion.

Anyway, his first terrorist act, a suicide bombing, went down like this. We drove in a '65 Buick Le Sabre convertible, a limping "boat" that was given to him by an admirer who observed that, "Someone with your ambitions needs a set of wheels." This was doubly good news for him because he could get to strategic sites, and now the car bomb thing was an option.

When we arrived, there was a bus in the mostly empty parking lot of a shopping mall "anchored" by a Target. ("Comical," I thought, "a terrorist target called Target. Let no one say he lacks a sense of humor.") The bus was full of old people, antiques, escapees from the local Home for the Bewildered, or, if you insist, "older Americans." (You can't even say "senior citizen" these days without inspiring some level of PC frowning followed by threats to "interrogate your socio-discursive orientation.") It was as if an assisted-living home had sent its residents out on a field trip described in that week's activity post as "Terrorism Today: Join a real terrorist plot in action! See what they do and how they do it. Activities to follow." And why not send them out on such a field trip? Why not be on the site of a terrorist attack that they could then read about in the newspaper the next morning? I say, let them have a little excitement, for God's sake.

Which is not to say that they were under any illusions. These "older Americans" seemed to understand that my friend was a suicide bomber and not a magician or a yoga instructor or a health professional there to teach them the Heimlich maneuver. They even seemed aware that he wanted to blow the bus up. I won't say they were happy to learn this, but they didn't seem to want to do anything about it either. They just sat there muttering about young people today and how much worse the world was going to be when they died. One old man—with a face like an old wrinkled sphincter—spat out that after he was gone the world wouldn't exist at all. He said, "After me—kaput!" It was true that his wasted and tattered legs did make the world seem precarious. Perhaps it *is* getting ready to collapse. My terrorist friend thought so. Even so, it surprised me that no one tried to escape from the bus (with the exception of a limping fellow with a broken umbrella who scutted across the asphalt like an injured bat pushed by the wind).

Old people. Who knows what they're thinking.

Anyway, the Terrorist and I started working on the bomb straight away. He got a propane stove going and put a pot of water on to boil. I was down by the door with a small pig—a piglet I think they're called—gutting the revolting thing and handing the entrails up to the Terrorist. It was a disgusting, gizzardy goulash, and it smelled deadly enough, that's for sure. Maybe this concoction really would kill people. What did I know? *He* was the terrorist.

The Terrorist put the pig guts in the kettle and a thick fatty smoke reeking to heaven began to rise up into something that looked like a parachute or a hot air balloon. According to him, when it reached maximum "potency," it would explode and send us all to kingdom come, the universe with us, just as that superannuated homunculus had suggested.

Anyway, there was no driver on the bus and no keys in the ignition and so we never moved from the parking lot, never even got close to the "Target." This was all part of the perennial sense of inadequacy that hounded my Terrorist. Even if we had been able to get close to the Target with our pig bomb, it was still a pretty crummy objective in comparison with, say, an Afghani police academy graduation ceremony, something that real terrorists, his comrades in the Middle East, could boast of. I suppose detonating the residents of a nursing home was supposed to be a consolation for a lowly American terrorist lacking meaningful targets, but they didn't fit the bill for me because they already seemed a bit sick of it all, close to saying, "Let's get this over with," so maybe we were doing them a favor.

The bomb making dragged on for some time and I got distracted talking to some geezer in coveralls and a filthy DeKalb seed cap down in the bus's stairwell. He said that he had once owned a Buick, too, back in his speckled youth, and that his friends called it "The Bomb." He thought that was pretty funny, given the circumstances. Lost in this ridiculous thought, I had mostly forgotten why we were there, when BANG!

The bomb went off with the kind of force you might expect from a Roy Rogers air rifle, and so, obviously, the bus was still there and all the aged losers in it. Perhaps some of the old timers were coughing or wheezing a little, but what else would an old person be doing even without the haze from a pig bomb? I looked up and all I could see was that, above the pot, the hot air balloon had punctured and there was a small charcoal smudge on the ceiling. The Terrorist was standing there a little singed and sooty. He looked like he was about to cry. He had been so excited about this and now it had amounted to nothing. He felt ridiculous.

After that, there didn't seem to be anything more to do, so we began to leave. Someone shouted, "Hey, aren't you going to clean up this mess?" and just as we reached the door an old lady in her old lady shawl and her old lady hat said, "I hope you young men are proud of yourselves!" The terrorist glared at her, and I was offended for his sake. He was new at this. Give him a break, I thought. So I reached down into the pig bucket and threw what was left of the

carcass at her, knocking off her tatty bonnet. The Terrorist stared a
hole right through me, as if he thought I had gone beyond my job
description: I blow things up, he thought, you watch.

"Just trying to help out, bro'," I pleaded.

But he really was disappointed, especially in himself. How
impotent he had been when the game was on the line. How could he
not be reminded of his father's hurtful nickname for him: Idiot, as in,
"Tell that idiot to mow the lawn. See if Idiot can change the oil in the
Caddy, or re-shingle the roof," or whatever kids used to do for their
fifty-cent allowance.

A digression concerning his father. His dad's head exploded from
natural causes when the Terrorist was just ten-years-old. In the weeks
leading up to this awful event, his father's head had swollen up as
if Lucifer's red-hot tick were sucking blood up through the straw of
his neck. When the Terrorist's alarmed mother commented on the
startling change, his father said, "You worry too much." Afterwards,
the physician assured her that she bore no blame and that the
progression of the illness was "textbook."

Anyway, he witnessed his dad's exploding noggin and was
never able to forget the image: skull fragments and purplish brain
matter whipping toward the walls. Behind him there was a shadow
on the wall created by his own body as the gore flew by. The poor kid
was never able to lose the sense that anything could blow up for no
reasonable reason at all, a purely arbitrary flick of our barbaric God's
finger, as if Our Father were merely getting snot off a finger.

It is possible that his father's death inspired him in a wicked
way. It inspired him to think that if his father's head, of all things,
could explode, then everything, Reality, was far from shatterproof and
it was his job to reveal the fact. If you'll excuse my lay analysis, his
version of terrorism was a form of OCD, a compulsive repetition of the
traumatic death of the father.

Sorry for the detour.

As we walked back to the Buick, it occurred to me that he
might be in no condition to drive home. I worried that he was so
disappointed that he might do something rash. Drive the car off a
bridge, turn into oncoming traffic, plow into an oak tree, like any
humdrum drunk driver. I was walking a little ahead of him, so I

turned and said, "Give me the keys." He looked at me and frowned, shrugged, and handed them over. I suppose you could say that I was a suicide bombing designated driver.

I put the top down on the Le Sabre and handed him an iconic black flag that he stuck out into the wind like a child with a whirligig, cheering him immeasurably.

The Terrorist's Idea for a Reality TV Show

"It is the duty of every patriot to hate his country creatively."
—Pursewarden, in Lawrence Durrell's Balthazar

A good part of what was so discouraging about this first attempt at a suicide bombing was that the Terrorist had decided to do it only with great difficulty. Decision-making actually caused him physical pain. Gun in one hand, pipe bomb in the other, I have seen him waste precious minutes looking back and forth, unable to determine which would provide "the more beautiful gesture." So, it was a remarkable thing when he firmly decided, "a lone actor, on a bus, with the viscera bomb."

Frustratingly, that had not worked out, as you know, and I was very worried about the consequences for him personally as well as for his vocational advancement, not to mention my own hopes for a book deal.

But then one day the Terrorist said he had an idea for a reality TV show that could ignite the last war of prophecy.

I was delighted.

"Good deal," I said, "but which prophecy is this?"

"The Prophecy of the Heavenly Twins."

He smiled ironically.

"I don't know that one."

It sounded like something he'd picked up on a porn site.

Anyway, he said he needed me to go with him to some L.A. production company and help sell the idea. Frankly, I think he just wanted me to drive again. Since the bus fiasco, I had become a sort of chauffeur for him. He couldn't afford gas for the hulking Buick, and

I think he liked the idea that my little Prius was not contributing to global warming as I ferried him from one terrorist activity to another. I suppose that I was not only a designated driver, but a terrorist soccer mom as well.

I may not have been burning much fuel, but I was burning vacation time at my job with the lofty X-Anathan Corporation. I whined some about that, not that I didn't have vacation time coming, and he asked, "What is this job of yours anyway?"

"Do you think that I am important enough that they would tell me? What kind of place do you take it for? This is the X-Anathan company, lofty X-Anathan, that you ask about!"

Anyway, under a lot of supervisory frowning, I did take some vacation time that I'd banked years earlier. It wasn't until I assured my manager that I could still perform micro-tasks on my phone, checking it every fifteen minutes, that the straight-ahead, brows-darkened frowning became a mere sneer of masterful contempt. But I was determined to take the time off because when the Terrorist finally did something worthy of terror, when he finally got around to killing a few people, I needed to be there…so I drove.

Eventually, we arranged to sit down with some studio guys, the much-maligned "suits" of TV-land. The Terrorist asked me to make the presentation because he was above speaking to such people. I said, "My friend's show is called 'Suburban Psychotic.' It is a weekly reality show based upon the antics of average Americans with mental illnesses. The premise is that four people—two men, two women, one black, one Asian, one Mexican, one white devil, but no Muslims, for that is forbidden—come to live in a house in Malibu. The opening theme song (an electric guitar playing something with that signature Ventures twang) should be put over scenes of healthy, tanned surfer boys and bikini-clad supermodels also from a politically correct range of races and ethnicities. That, I hope, goes without saying. Next, we cut to the suffocating interior of the house and all the depressing filth and torn curtains, piles of pizza boxes, and empty diet Coke bottles.

"That sets the scene.

"Our contestants all suffer from various psychological conditions. For example, there could be a paranoid schizophrenic, a category one bipolar in the manic state, one psychotic with anal obsessions (especially for anuses other than his own), and, for the purpose of developing a more traditional demographic among our viewers, a feeb, a pinhead, a moron, or an idiot. You know, the coo-coos from back when a mental illness and a malicious slur were the same thing; back when the insane were stored in vast stone manors where they leaked vile fluids and did a lot of muttering. But the point is—crazy people. A variety pack of crazy people. And naturally the contestants may be insane, but they are all young studs and hotties."

"God is Great!" shouted the Terrorist, startling the hell out of the media bigwigs.

"Of course, all four contestants are on powerful psycho-active drugs, but my friend's idea is that for the duration of the season we take away their meds. One other crucial thing, there's a pistol in a glass box in the middle of the kitchen table. Just one. The contestants, of course, will soon begin to eye it with envy, worried that one of the housemates will use it first. In the course of the television season, the show's 'losers' will try to commit suicide with this gun. They are our winners, our great 'American Losers.' We will say that they have 'Won the Gun,' a meme that social media will be sure to pick up giving the program plenty of free advertising. The show's many fans will append WTG to their own desperate suicidal tweets. The sole remaining contestant will live on even if the director and camera crew have to wrestle the pistol away from him or her. Picture it: a suicidal babe in a hot pink halter top—halting nothing much of her expansive bosom—wrestled to the ground by a supporting crew of lusty young dudes, sleeves rolled up above fierce tattoos, their strong hands possessing her morose but nonetheless appetizing flesh.

At this point one of the studio honchos interrupted me and said, "This is starting to come together for me. What would you think if this rescue of the winner/loser by the crew included last second appearances of the winner's childhood sweetheart, or a lost brother, a favorite high school math teacher, etc. Or perhaps we could use someone that the winner idolizes, there to offer support and encouragement? A favorite sports star? You know, a Tom Brady lookalike rushes in from the wings. Or an unrequited high school crush played by a tearful Sasha Grey, all leggy hope for the future, saying something like, 'You were always my true love!'"

The Terrorist looked at him in haughty disdain and interjected, "I think I would take my concept to another producer, that's what I'd think."

"Okay, okay, just playing with this idea of yours. How about if we had the winner's estranged father save him?"

The Terrorist looked as if he had been turned into a wax figure of himself, his mouth in a rictus of scorn.

"What's the matter with him?" the studio guy asked.

I interceded. "Please don't mention fathers to him. He is a little sensitive on that point."

"Oh, sorry, I understand. Anyone would understand. My father is dead, so I'm fortunate. I suppose his is still mucking about."

"Not exactly."

I turned back to the Terrorist and said, encouragingly, "It's okay, my friend. Shall I go on?"

He nodded darkly.

"To conclude, this last scene is accompanied by happy tears, with the exception, of course, of the winning contestant who will be put in restraints.

"The survivor will be spirited away to a vacation rehab facility on the island of Maui run by the NSA where a thorough review of his or her drug protocol will be conducted by top professionals in the field, after which the winner will go on with his or her miserable sham of a life, emotionally flat lined."

That was it. The execs nodded judiciously and said it was an interesting concept. They said that we might just be on to something new. The industry was always looking for the next big thing. I heard that a pilot was made and that FX was taking it seriously. As for the messianic effects foretold by the terrorist—that million year caliphate thing?—I don't know, I haven't seen him in a while.

Five Poems

from field recordings of mind in morning

☆

Hank Lazer

field recordings   of mind   in morning

who can say   what remains
this is the song   of what you say

i live in the present moment of my reading
i live in the present moment of my writing

& each becomes a way

8/21/19

this is different
here   where i can see &   be with them

when & where thinking &
writing
happen in the same
moment

a cloudy morning   fog at dawn

a startled doe awakens from
sleeping beneath a cedar tree &
runs heavy & hard into
the woods

as he averred   in a study of the word
thinking & thanking

this restorative morning

                    8/22/19
                    Duncan Farm

don't lose what is happening to you this morning

they were wanderers out of necessity
my father's parents left Russia
(or is it now Lithuania)
crossed Siberia by train
(ten days i was told)
met up with relatives in Harbin
then moved to Yokohama
& eventually moved to the small farming town of
San José California
where my father was born in 1926

we always lived nearby   within walking distance
& saw them every week   Fanya & Chaim

each had a calmness & steadiness that
they seemed unaware of

some true ancestors we get to know
in the slow practice
of being's unfolding

8/25/19

why bother with the transport of words

when there is this
adequacy & intricacy
of specific fact

one could call it   flat actuality
but that
isn't it either

as messengers
in different rhythms

in spite of
odd pauses
it's a singing that
goes on & on

8/31/19
Duncan Farm

"such echoes   of heaven on earth"

three brown dogs   absolutely at rest
after a walk & a run
the young one   full of speed
tail quivering   moving quickly
throughout
70 acres of pasture

early morning sunlight
moment by moment
intricate & particular
upon the treeline & small hillside

meditation & writing   beside
the dogs' steady & easeful breathing

i abide here Bob
with your "endlessly present talking"
much lIke
breath   or light

9/1/19
Duncan Farm

Everlasting Duration

in memory of George

☆

Rochelle Owens

You are sitting down
to a late lunch
in my castle on a hill

while a jazz trio plays

then suddenly
a chemical reaction
takes place---

and you smell
the scent of roses and feel
my hair growing

on every part of your skin

but not the palms
of my hands or the soles
of your feet

Day One

I am standing
in front of a group of musicians
controlling

the speed of sound

then suddenly
a chemical reaction
takes place---

saliva pools behind
your teeth   sinuous the rhythms
under my skin

your lips move

audible   inaudible
and I begin to chant a secret
tribal language

Day Two

In a triangle of haze
and smoke I am following
a marching band

appear and disappear

then suddenly
a chemical reaction
takes place---

spirals of veins pulsate
nerves and tendons drink color
sight   smell   taste

pale and red your lips

my tongue protrudes
from your mouth and I taste
the rain

Day Three

You are hanging
upside down and side to side
I swing

earth   air   fire   water

then suddenly
a chemical reaction
takes place---

I am a barley plant
cut down   dead white the barley
plant cut down

you are a pouched mammal

attached to a nipple
mother and father crawled
onto the land

Day Four

I am flapping
my right hand and your left
hand is balled into a fist

the universe contracts   e x p a n d s

then suddenly
a chemical reaction
takes place---

the smell of saffron
and lilac   morning to evening
evening to morning

milk of the mother misery

milk of the father terror
vigilant the babe   sucking   carnal/
spiritual

Day Five

Through the gaps
of my fingers vibrating subatomic
particles blink in and out

vertical/ horizontal

then suddenly
a chemical reaction
takes place---

a breast vein
as thick as a finger   amorous
the greedy seed

every day bears the data

grain   grape   bread
and wine   your skeletal frame
the limbs spreading apart

Day Six

Behind you
a black line appears   disappears
a latent image

a wall of brown dust

then suddenly
a chemical reaction
takes place---

a black line curved
like an embrace   lay your hand
feel the bones

under my skin

your sculpted pelvis
vertical/ horizontal   corkscrews
of white smoke

Day Seven

In the twenty-first century
the here-and-now   in the zone
diverging

from a course of events

then suddenly
a chemical reaction takes
place---

a metallic taste on
my tongue   I am an old
woman

sipping black tea

you are a little boy
sitting cross-legged under
a dead blue glow

Europe

☆

John Olson

May, 1972. I sat in a chair staring at a large glass wall somewhere at the Los Angeles Airport. Anna sat next to me. We were waiting to board a chartered plane to take us to England. We had no real plan other than to put ourselves in Europe and see what happens. We hoped that some opportunity for generating income would present itself. It was easy finding a place to live in the 1970s, at least in the United States and even better in Europe. That's what we were thinking: a better quality of life in Europe away from the aggressive commercialism of unfettered capitalism in a culture that exalted wealth above all things and ruined a landscape of forests and lakes and rivers and prairies with freeways and shopping malls. It was brutish and wasteful and soul-shriveling-swinish and we wanted out.

It was crazy. Neither of us had any real plan. We'd read all of Kate's letters from Spain and France with great excitement and envy and saw how easily she managed to get by.

How did she get by? That's a question that occurs to me now, 47 years later, sitting on a bed typing these words on a laptop. I worry a great deal about money and savings and ways to generate income if social security is destroyed by a corrupt, thuggish, corporatized government.

Brigitte and I (we've been married for 25 years) budget

ourselves very strictly. We inhabit a world very different than the one that existed in the 1970s. This world is much harsher, much less forgiving. People are bankrupted by an extortionate healthcare system. There are tent cities everywhere, along freeways and by freeway entrances, under bridges, on downtown sidewalks. There is everywhere the stench of urine, deposits of fecal matter, and syringes and needles carelessly tossed aside. Forty percent of Americans cannot afford an unexpected expense of $400 dollars or more, and 40 percent of Americans cannot afford one basic need such as rent, medical bills, or food.

Meanwhile, one individual – Jeff Bezos – owns more wealth than the 3.5 billion below the median average wealth. Bezos has a wealth of 165.6 billion dollars. An average worker in one of his warehouses makes $14.00 dollars an hour and is lucky if they get a bathroom break. Fourteen an hour is roughly (before taxes and social security are taken out) $1,840 a month. The average rent for a one-bedroom apartment in Seattle is $1,968. This means that even working a full shift you'd have to share an apartment. Which is going to prevent you from starting a family. All you do is work. You have no future. At least, no future with a spouse and children and a stable income. You will have a future of climate change and flooding and hurricanes and tornados and mass shootings almost daily. Sorry for the buzz kill I'm just describing things in a general sense. Individually, our worlds are going to enriched according to our resources – our resourcefulness - and our imagination.

And hey, marijuana is legalized for recreational use in ten states. Other pharmaceuticals, however, such as Daraprim, for the treatment of toxoplasmosis and cystoisosporiasis, is $45,000 for one month. Actimmune, which is used to boost the immune system in chronic granulomatous disease, is a whopping $52,321.80 for one month.

The world was a much more benign place in the 1970s. There was still a little residual effect from the movements and cultural rebellion of the 60s hanging in the air, and the middle-class was robust and ubiquitous. Salaries were even. Unions were strong. When people took the bus or train or a passenger jet they were treated with dignity and respect. No one was surveilled, unless they were wanted by the police, or suspected of crime. People sat on benches and chairs reading magazines and books. They were informed. They thought about things. Conversations could go places, often amazing places, surprising the very people conversing at the swirl of ideas and possibilities they generated. You didn't see people walking down a sidewalk gazing mindlessly at a handheld computer.

But still. To get on a plane and go to Europe for an indefinite amount of time with nothing solid mapped out was something akin to the fool on the Tarot card, a good-looking guy in a colorful, skirted tunic carrying a stick with a bag dangling from the end, a dog barking joyfully and excitedly as the Fool approaches the edge of a cliff, insouciant and merry, paying no attention at all to his immediate surroundings, holding a white flower with his other hand, seconds before he goes plummeting into the abyss. It's comical. And it's tragic.

And that was me. Anna had a clearer idea of our financial situation and this would be a constant worry for her and a source of anger that I didn't share her concern.

We'd spent several months in Seattle staying with my parents. That had been very generous of them. It allowed me an opportunity to make some money before we left. I got a job painting with an outfit on Eastlake below the Eastlake Zoo, one of the funkiest taverns I'd ever been in where you can sit upstairs and smoke dope. The clientele all looked like members of ZZ Top. I painted a motorcycle repair shop in Bellevue a bright fluorescent orange, and a huge billboard overlooking a used car lot with a solid white background.

We flew to Los Angeles to catch our charter plane. At Sea-Tac, I spotted a tall guy that looked familiar and thought at first he was someone I knew from high school. But I couldn't place him. Then I realized it was the actor Donald Sutherland. He was with Jane Fonda. They'd just been filming *Klute*, which takes place in New York. I can't remember why they were in Seattle. Maybe they'd filmed a scene or two in Vancouver, BC.

Anna went to call her mother in San José to let her know how we were and that we were about to fly to LA. She made the call from a bank of public phones, each phone with its own small booth. Apart from us, the only other person making a call was Jane Fonda, who popped out and asked if I could watch her luggage while she made a dash to the cocktail lounge a few feet away. I said sure. Her luggage looked expensive, hand-tooled leather. The phone dangled.

I wondered if her dad was on the other end. Jane returned and thanked me and to back on the phone. Turns out she and Donald were on the same flight to LA with us. Every time I got up to go to the bathroom I had to squeeze past Donald who spent nearly the entire flight standing in the aisle talking to the other passengers. He's a very tall man. I envied the guy Jane sat next to. What a surprise that must've been. Jane is a very talkative and affable woman.

This was the first time I'd been to LA. I didn't get to see much of it. Just the airport. And the gray mist on the other side of the immense glass wall. The future. Foreign lands. Adventure.

Finally, the time came to board our plane. Everyone in this section of the airport was waiting for the chartered plane to London, England. We made a line and showed our tickets and everyone got seated, sorted things out, luggage tucked away, and after the flight attendants went up and down the aisles making sure everyone's seatbelt was buckled the plane began to move and taxi out to the tarmac and then – karunch! - hit a building. The tip of the right wing crumpled. The plane sat there for a few minutes and an announcement was made that the plane would return to the gate and everyone would disembark and wait while the plane was repaired.

And we did. And we waited. A group of people became very disgruntled and had some words with a booking agent with the charter company and it was decided that the charter service would give us lunch and put us up in a motel.

An hour or so later Anna found ourselves in a motel room watching a Danny Kaye movie.

* * * * *

I remember gazing out of the plane window at the Arctic below. Pure white for as far as I could see. The last time I flew over the Arctic – in January, 2015 – the Arctic looked slushy and mottled and rapidly disappearing.

We landed at Heathrow airport, disembarked on the tarmac, and were led into a small building. While we were standing there, a policeman or security or drug agent of some sort in a dark blue uniform began chatting with me. He immediately broached the subject of drugs, hashish in particular for some reason. I was happy to tell him all about it. Yes, I'd tried it. But I didn't care for it. It made me paranoid. After a little more conversation, it became apparent to him that I really didn't care about cannabis or any other drug I just wanted to see Europe. And he went on his way and started a conversation with someone else. I missed him. I liked talking to him.

*   *   *   *   *

I remember standing in a London street, finishing a cigarette and not knowing where to put it out. I felt like I was standing in a museum. The whole city felt like a museum. The buildings were different than the buildings in America, not all of them, but a few of them, enough of them to give the feeling of being elsewhere, not just in space, but in time. I was in the country of poets like Keats and Shelley. Lord Byron's antics and flamboyance. Oscar Wilde going by in a cape with a mischievous smile.

The difficulty of finding a good breakfast. Of finding real food anywhere. People in England didn't seem to have any understanding or appreciation of food. I ordered pancakes in one restaurant and there wasn't any syrup provided. Just a mound of sugar on top of my pancakes. Which tasted like rubber.

I remember standing in line for the British museum. The people next to us in line were older and were from the north and were far friendlier than the people of London.

I remember seeing a glass case full of letters by Lady Elgin, Vladimir Lenin, Percy Bysshe Shelley and one by George Bernard Shaw written insultingly and specifically for museum goers pondering such letters that this pursuit was a foolish and shallow enterprise and a colossal misuse of time. I felt like flipping it off. "Mama, why is that man flipping off a letter?"

I cooled off and restored my self-esteem elsewhere in the museum by gazing at clay tablets of cuneiform writing and hundreds of other ancient and historic items. Spears, swords, shields. A skullcap from Borneo. A Klickitat spoon from the Willamette Valley. The latter was particularly intriguing. It was odd and strangely moving to see something from home on display in England.

The muscle-attachment areas of a set of Anglo-Saxon skeletal remains revealed what was once an extremely robust physique and a hat from the Nicobar Islands made of stems from a coconut tree tickled my fancy.

I was both surprised and galvanized at hearing so many English dialects. One of the oddest accents I heard was from a young man with long thick red hair sitting on a grassy knoll in Hyde Park. I asked what part of England he was from and he said Alabama.

I remember hitchhiking to Dover and spending the night at Mote Park in Maidstone. A kind and enthusiastic young man we met while buying some fish and chips helped us find the park and regaled us with a brief survey of the town's main features and conveniences. We went into a local pub for cigarettes and ale and a group of young men sitting at a table and a little bit drunk began making fun of my American accent. The young man acting as our guide ushered us out of the pub as quickly as possible.

I remember waiting for the ferry in Dover and a plainclothes policeman convinced that we were carrying hashish. He smelled Anna's suede handbag. We explained that a bottle of patchouli oil had come open and leaked all over the purse. We showed him her purse and he seemed disappointed that he hadn't found any hashish.

I remember catching a ride with a couple of guys from Canada, one of whom was Quebecois, who were driving a large van. We crossed the English Channel with them. We waited a long time at the dock in Calais while the French police went over the van very carefully. In retrospect, I count it very lucky these guys weren't carrying any drugs.

I remember the drive to Paris and how flat the Norman countryside was and full of farms it reminded me a great deal of the American Midwest. The Canadians picked up three or four young French adults who were hitchhiking and a couple of guys from Liverpool who were total assholes. They joked about French frogs and seemed to be visiting France with the sole purpose of making fun of them. We stopped to get gas and I uttered my first French words (*où sont les toilettes?*) and went to the men's room in the gas station which was exactly like any other men's room at a gas station I'd ever been in and when I was on my way out and went to the door one of the Liverpool guys smashed the door into me. I think he was spoiling for a fight. I ignored it and gave him the stink eye and went to the van. The young men of England seem to be spoiling for fights a lot. Now I know why Shakespeare put so many fights in his plays.

I remember entering Paris and how crowded it seemed.

It was teeming with life. London had seemed so orderly. Paris, by comparison, was rather chaotic, but full of color and a gazillion different things and types of food to discover. The coffee was fantastic. Their crepes were out of this world. You didn't have to go to a restaurant the crepes were made at little stands on the sidewalk and were everywhere. There were people doing card tricks and swallowing fire and blowing flames out of their mouth and some Arabs showed us a knife.

I remember going to the bathroom at a restaurant. The men's room was downstairs and after I relieved myself the lights went off. I panicked and shouted and a waiter came down and flipped the lights on. I felt embarrassed.

* * * * *

We continued hitchhiking south and made it to Avignon where I came down with the flu. This meant we had to get a hotel room for a couple of days. These expenses were beginning to weigh heavily on Anna and cause increasing tension in our relationship.

Funny word, 'relationship.' 'Relate' is from Latin *relationem* (nominative *relatio*), and referring to "a bringing back, restoring; a report, proposition."

A relationship is a constant bringing back, trying always to repair the damages and wear caused by natural attrition, but also flares of anger, irritations expressed that concuss into irritations from your partner, all this has to be mended, patched, brought back from the shadows into the light of calmer emotion and truer feeling, original feeling, which requires a report, a telling, a narrative and yes, above all a continuing proposition. An entreaty, a supplication, a plea.

And that final word, 'ship.' You do everything you can to keep it all afloat. To keep it headed somewhere, an island, an archipelago, coconuts and treasures, white sands and iridescent coral, cool streams and nourishing tropical fruits and flowers.

Or just aim for the horizon, that ever alluring wraith of mist in the distance. The tingle of moisture on the skin, sails clattering in the wind, bulging with it, those insane hopes, that invisible spirit that animates everything from the snail to the beluga whale.

I lie in bed with a French comic book I was using to help me learn the language. Almost all of it I found hopelessly confusing and didn't have a dictionary so I went back to reading the selected poetry of William Blake I'd brought. I gazed out the window and saw a gypsy van. It reminded me of the print of Van Gogh's gypsy wagons I had pinned to the wall of my room at the Arcata Hotel.

And I thought of Jef Rosman's oil painting of Arthur Rimbaud, miserable in bed, a sorrowful head reposing on two pillows, after his friend and lover Paul Verlaine shot him in the wrist with a small 7 mm Lefaucheux revolver.

This little gun still exists. It sold recently for £368,000 at auction at Christie's in Paris.

The gun is historic for other reasons as well. Its inventor, Casimir Lefaucheux, is credited with introducing the first truly efficient self-contained cartridge system which featured a pin-fire mechanism. The cartridge used a conical bullet, a cardboard powder tube, and a copper base that incorporated a primer pellet, thus making it one of the first practical breech-loading weapons. It became the first metallic-cartridge revolver adopted by a national government.

If a gun doesn't kill you, time will. I've always liked that expression, "killing time." Nice to have a little occasional revenge before the inevitable arrives.

Time is such a weird thing. There's really no true linearity to it. It doesn't actually travel like an arrow from one place to another. Time moves relative to our perspective. There is no future. There is no past. There is only this present, which has great elasticity, thanks to words, which are the mules here dragging it back and forth over the landscape, which is pixels on a laptop screen.

* * * * *

We hitched a ride into Arles and spent the night at a youth hostel. Men and women had to sleep in separate quarters, even if you were married. That was weird, but it was only one night.

I remember seeing my first Roman amphitheater. A man wearing a straw hat was selling Van Gogh prints and memorabilia.

The amphitheater was built in 90 AD and was capable of seating over 20,000 spectators. It's first spectacle was Wings with Paul and Linda McCartney and Denny Laine.

Or maybe it was Queen doing "Bohemian Rhapsody."

Or gladiators. Probably gladiators.

We wandered around an antique store and woman saw me holding a little saucepan and said "*il est en cuivre.*" I thought about buying it, but our backpacks were already stuffed to the gills. I had fantasies of Vincent Van Gogh boiling water in it.

We hitched a ride down to Sainte-Marie-la-Mer where a gypsy festival was in progress. This was the Gitan Pilgrimage, a celebration and ceremony that takes place each year between May 24th and May 25th to honor the three Marys, St. Marie-Jacobé, St. Marie-Salomó and Sara la-Kali (aka Black Sara, aka the Black Madonna) the patron saint of the gypsies. According to legend, the three Marys arrived at this place by boat from Palestine and were given refuge. Two rows of men on white stallions, wearing black hats and carrying lances, provide a guard of honor for a statuette of Saint Sara, wrapped in gold cloth and carried on a four-handled palette down to the Mediterranean where she is doused with water. People crowd around cheering and chanting "Vive Sainte Sara!" as musicians play flamenco guitar or Hungarian melodies on accordion and musette de cour.

I visited the cathedral where the doll of Saint Sara is kept in a cellar heated by hundreds of candles. She reposes in a niche where people bring prayers and wishes written on paper and leave gifts and offerings. I remember how warm it was in there, and holy and strange.

Until the climactic moment of the ceremony when the four horsemen ride down to the shore of the Mediterranean with the effigy of Saint Sara, the festival resembles any other festival I've attended, with booths of food and handcrafted items for sale.

Anna and I encountered another American couple wandering around, the writer Jerry Hopkins and his wife. Hopkins, who would later produce a book about his friend Jim Morrison titled *No One Here Gets Out Alive*, that was used as the basis for Oliver Stone's 1991 movie about The Doors, was writing an article about the festival for *Rolling Stone*. Jerry and his wife invited us to their hotel room where I saw Jerry's article in the typewritor (and would read it in a copy of the *Rolling Stone* several months later) and then took us out to dinner. I corresponded with Jerry a few months before losing touch. He passed away in Bangkok, Thailand in 2018 at age 82 after a long illness.

* * * * *

We continued hitching south until we arrived in Barcelona, not quite sure what to do. I vaguely remember a young man accompanying us, but what I do remember in a vividness that still makes me nervous when I think back on it, is losing sight of Anna. I had some vague idea of where she was headed, but this was our first day in the city and I didn't know squat about where I was or where to go or what to do. In a panic, I approached a phalanx of police or soldiers, I wasn't sure what they were, what their official status was, but Francisco Franco was still in charge in his role as caudillo, a man with both military and political power. In short, a Fascist dictator. There seemed to be a lot of gradations of police, some carrying machine guns, like the ones I approached, it's a miracle they didn't shoot me. I asked one of them for the direction of a street and as he motioned toward me with an answer he was shouted back into ranks by an officer and I apologized and walked away feeling bad I'd gotten him into trouble. Minutes later I spotted Anna and I ran to greet her. She seemed almost irritated that I'd found her.

There'd been a lot friction between us and it was fast spiraling out of control. The trip to Europe had been a disaster for our relationship.

Anna's mood improved a little when a group of fellow Americans told us about a coastal town to the north that attracted a lot of tourists in the summer. It was a bigtime party town. It sounded fun, and there might be an opportunity to find some sort of job there. Maybe. My resolve to figure out a way to generate income and make it possible to live in France or Spain had been overwhelmed by the sensory overload of being in a foreign country and the myriad, unexpected problems in trying to live on the cheap, camping out much of the time, which is exhausting. Lloret de Mar seemed like it might offer a little stability, a place to rest and think about what to do. This turned out to be quite the opposite.

I loved Lloret de Mar. Almost as soon as we arrived, I began drinking. Drinks were cheap. Accommodations were cheap. This made it possible to spend a little more extravagantly on booze. Not a good move on my part. Not at all. I stayed riotously drunk for two weeks.

We fell in with a group of Scotsmen who all worked in restaurants and shared a large apartment. They let us come and do laundry and we all sat at a big round table playing gin rummy while the Scots had me in stiches with their wry humor. It was so much easier to make friends with the Scots than the English. It seemed that further south you went in England, the more proper and stand-offish the people became. The further north, the warmer the people were.

I did have trouble understanding much of what was said, particularly in the noisy confines of a bar. I got tired of constantly asking the Scots to repeat themselves and so began to smile and pretend I understood and appreciated what they were saying.

Lloret de Mar reminded me a great deal of my time in Arcata. Everything was within easy walking distance. There was one guy I remember, a fellow American who always wore a trench coat, even when it was hot, drove a scooter. One night he'd gotten so plastered that he toppled over in a vacant lot and slept next to the scooter, the warmth of the engine feeling snug as a companion dog. Nights by the Mediterranean could get chilly.

Some of the discos didn't open until 3:00 a.m. The people in this town took partying to a whole new level

Two weeks was sufficient to realize that my evolution toward income-generation was stillborn. A much larger monster had been born: incipient alcoholism.

We left Lloret de Mar by bus. I left feeling quite uncomfortable, mainly because I'd had to take a monster dump and went to the men's room. An ancient woman in a black shawl (women in black shawls seemed to be everywhere in Spain) sat in the alcove knitting something. She had a roll of toilet paper on her lap. I thought she must be a crazy person. I entered the bathroom and on a suspicion checked for toilet paper in the stalls. There was none. Now I understood. I went back out and approached the old woman and pointed at the roll of toilet paper on her lap. She tore off a section and asked for three or four pesetas, I can't remember. I don't know why I didn't bargain for more, but I took the little panel of tissue into the bathroom and made do with that. I'm sure it was fine, I didn't have diarrhea, thank god, but I tend to be very OCD about hygiene.

There's a very uptight Jack Lemon behind all this bohemian façade.

* * * * *

  We took a bus to Perpignan, France, and arrived very late at night. We got off at the train station. A single man stood on the quay, a taxi driver. He could see immediately by our backpacks that we were hitchhiking our way through Europe and could use some help. He said he had a brother who let people stay at his house. I thought that was remarkable, but worried that this might be a trap of some sort. Maybe his brother traps stray tourists in his cellar and sticks them in a freezer and eats them for breakfast. But we were extremely tired and disoriented and so said yes, oui, that would be very nice. He drove to us a nice house, not terribly big but certainly spacious enough, and lo and behold it did indeed have a spare room for guests and the man's brother turned out to be quite genteel, or *gentil,* as they French say. He took me into the bathroom and (he didn't speak any English at all) motioned that I could take a shower. *Douche! Douche!* He said. I felt too vulnerable in the circumstances and tried to take him up on that. I just wanted to crawl into bed. I told him that maybe I would in the morning, *le matin, peut-être,* I said.

  The next day I paid the man a small sum of money, five francs I think, and he gave us a small breakfast of coffee and croissants and gave us directions on how to get to D118, the highway that went to Carcassonne, traveling through the beautiful countryside of the Aude with dreamlike villages steeped in medieval lore, lush vineyards and poplar-lined streams, occasional forests of beech and alder and ash and Cathar castles in the hills. In one village, while waiting to catch another ride, two women came up and although neither spoke a word of English communicated somehow that there was a festival in the village in progress and could they touch my hair, *puis-je toucher vos cheveux, monsieur?* Sure, I said, not at all sure as to why she wanted to touch my hair. Long hair must not have been in style there yet. Had we stumbled back in time to the 1890s? The woman touched my hair and laughed.

  Carcassonne was magnificent. It was huge. The fortress stands imposingly on a hill with massive double crenellated stone walls joined by 53 towers and barbicans to prevent attack by siege engines. Inside is an entire village and a Gothic cathedral,

Cathédrale Saint-Michel de Carcassonne. The streets are cobblestoned and narrow and I noticed little ruts grooved into them where garbage and sewage must've flowed.

We ate lunch at a restaurant with an outdoor patio and shared a table with a young American woman who astonished me with her ability to speak fluent French.

The next morning we hitched A709 to Orange, another town with a Roman amphitheater. We spent the night at a campground above the amphitheater and then caught a ride with a youngish, thirty-something couple who seemed eager to have our company. They spoke fluent English and we did our best to be conversational and lively which they seemed to appreciate. The man had some business to attend to in one little town and it felt good to be part of someone's regular life rather than the usual waiters and waitresses and hotel attendants that were part of the tourist industry. When we arrived in Cluny, we were able to get rooms at the same hotel and the couple bought us dinner at an elegant restaurant with thick white tablecloths. Using the various objects on the table the man gave me a lesson in demonstrative French pronouns, *ceci, cela, ceux-ci, ceux-là.* I had fun saying them and the man complemented me on my pronunciation. We thought we'd hit it off and expected to see the couple in the morning but they had already left. This gave me a somewhat uncomfortable feeling, but it wasn't a problem to catch a train for the rest of the way to Paris.

We boarded a passenger car, empty but for one elderly woman who smiled when we entered and sat down. She was poised and sophisticated in the special way that a French woman can be knowing and sympathetic, and when she noticed that we were struggling to figure out a map she politely intervened, asking if she could help us. We were very happy to receive her assistance. We grew quite friendly and as more people began to board the train we were joined by a young man who, as luck would have it, was as passionate about poetry as I was. We became friends immediately. He was more than happy to help me with my French. The seats were structured so that Anna and the elderly woman sat facing me and the young man with their back to the front of the train, which by now was extremely crowded.

Anna was locked in conversation with the old woman, whose name was Gabrielle Perrault, and who was a consultant for art galleries, chiefly in rural areas.

My new friend's name was Raphael Fontaine. We talked about Mallarmé. Mallarmé, we both emphatically agreed, was crucial to the development of innovative poetry. We both had the same sense that Mallarmé had moved everything forward, to a place where poetry needed to be, the vitality of the word, of language, of vital disconnect between words and the world, the chains of referentiality that kept language hidden from itself.

Literature was red hot with crisis. There was a revolution going on. It was happening in France and happening in the United States. It had begun with Baudelaire, who'd been influenced by Poe, long before Dada. Right around the time Rimbaud had quit poetry in disgust and took off for Africa Mallarmé took the reins and began promulgating ideas about writing that held it safely above the profane and made of it something chimerical and antagonistic to commerce. Too bad Rimbaud didn't stick around long enough to go to one of Mallarme's Tuesday evening soirées. He could've met Alfred Jarry. My god. What an encounter that would've been.

Raphael recently heard Maurice Blanchot lecture at the Sorbonne on Mallarmé and said it had been mind-blowing, *hallucinant.*

Are you familiar with Blanchot? he asked.

No, I had to admit, I hadn't heard of him. What did have to say about Mallarmé?

C'était étonnant. He said. Do you know *étonnant'* ?

Yes, astonishing, right ?

He said Mallarmé lived for language. His texts, always highly elliptical, were brilliant, but their meaning had to be ferreted out, like biblical parables, or zen koans. He allowed plenty of space for paradox and contradiction. He believed in two languages: the brute language of the everyday, rough and immediate, and the other essential, *débridé* – how do you say, without bridles in English? Unrestrained, I answered. *Oui, c'est ça,* unrestrained and polyvalent. In chemistry, a valent is the combining power of a substance. Mallarmé urged a poetics of great combinatory power, and for that he used the strategy of divagation. Do you know this word, divagation? Oh yeah, I said, I live for divagation.

Ah oui, moi aussi! Have you written much poetry?

No, not really. Nothing I consider really good. I struggle with it a lot.

Ce n'est pas facile, he said, smiling, knowingly. *Ce n'est pas facile.*

As we approached Paris, Raphael wrote down his home address and urged us to come and visit him the next afternoon. I said wow, sure, that'd be great. I told Anna, and she smiled, which made me greatly happy and relieved. I had not yet become someone she totally despised.

As we disembarked Raphael said goodbye, and had me say *à bientôt. À bientôt!* I exclaimed. I felt proud. It wasn't much, but I was speaking French.

* * * * *

In Paris, Gabrielle took us to her hotel to see if they might have a room available. It wasn't a luxury hotel, but it was quite nice and I could tell by the way the concierge looked at us that they weren't going to have a room available, which they did not. Gabrielle gave it her best, but the staff at the desk wouldn't relent. She asked us to wait in the lobby and after she got settled in her room and her luggage packed away she came down and took us out to find a hotel. We walked along the Pont des Arts and we stopped to look at Notre-Dame cathedral, which shown brightly in the night with flood lights on it.

Regardez! Gabrielle exclaimed. *Elle est belle !*

Oui, elle est très, très belle, I exclaimed. I was getting the hang of it. I liked speaking French.

Gabrielle found us a reasonably priced hotel and bid us goodbye and asked if we'd like to have coffee together in the morning.

Oh yes, that'd be lovely, said Anna.

During the night I got up and spent some time looking out of the window, marveling at the energy of the city. It was late, about 2 a.m., and yet lights were on and people were out roaming in the streets. I loved it. It was so unlike Seattle, or London, in which everyone went to bed early and the city closed up and there was nothing on the streets but fog and dreary reflections.

In London, we'd seen *The Ruling Class* with Peter O'Toole. There's a scene in which O'Toole lets out a deafening scream. Now I knew where that scream came from.

The French didn't hide their emotions. They let them out. Didn't matter whether the situation was appropriate or inappropriate. Appropriate and inappropriate are repressive terms for a repressive culture. The French didn't feel ashamed of what they were feeling, the intensity of the feeling or the propriety of the display. They valued spontaneity. An emotion was far less damaging and toxic if it was given free expression rather than buried in one's consciousness like a barrel of radioactive waste.

We met Gabrielle the next morning at Le Petit Café in the fifth arrondissement for croissants and coffee. We sat outside in the hugely pleasant sunny May morning. All the French restaurants had an outdoor space for eating. I don't know why they enjoy eating outdoors so much, but they sure do. Even during a cold January you'll see people outdoors eating, a few heat lamps keeping things reasonably comfortable, though I suspect a little wine and whiskey helped as well.

Gabrielle talked about how she got interested in art as a young girl. When she was thirteen, her father took her to see an art show of American art in Luxembourg in 1920 and it made a huge impression on her. She was especially impressed with the work of John Singer Sargent. Her father had worked as a salesman for a large hardware and building materials company in Dijon, but his first passion had been art. She attended *L'École nationale supérieure d'art de Dijon* but lacked the confidence to try and make a living as an artist. She discovered, instead, a flair for putting shows together and had a good eye for new and exciting art.

Anna said she'd really enjoyed the pre-Raphaelites at the Tate Museum. She especially like *The Lady Of Shalott* by John William Waterhouse.

I enthused over William Blake's miniature, *The Ghost of a Flea*, and Henry Fuseli's highly dramatic scenes touching on the supernatural and the macabre, such as *The Nightmare*, with the incubus sitting on the woman's chest. Fuseli favored the primacy of the imagination over realistic depiction and that had a strong appeal for me. I also really liked the contrast between light and dark in painting, such as the chiaroscuro in Rembrandt's *The Philosopher* and the candle flame rising to a point and disappearing into space in George de la Tour's *Magdalene with the Smoking Flame*. I love the way she sits, steeped in contemplation, it's exquisite, a fabulous moment, whoever this woman is, she could be anyone, staring at the candle flame next to a stack of books, cradling her chin in her right arm. Her thoughts are completely her own, but the darkness around her is something we all experience.

Oh I love George de la Tour, exclaimed Gabrielle. Did you know his work was virtually forgotten after his death in 1652. He wasn't rediscovered until 1934, when a few of his works were shown at the "Les Peintres de la Realité" exhibit of 1934, à l'orangerie. He made quite an impression on the people of that time, just as fascism was beginning to spread its shadow across Europe. People were starved for light, and a sense of transcendence, a feeling that the sublime was within reach. Do you know what I mean?

Yes, I do, I said.

We finished our breakfast and insisted on paying for everything and Gabrielle gave us a warm send-off. We watched as she walked down the Rue Descartes and disappeared into the crowd.

* * * * *

Anna and I spent several hours wandering the corridors of the Louvre looking for paintings by Vermeer. We found the correct place in the museum, but the Vermeers were being treated and restored, and not available for view. We lingered, instead, in the Italian section – Titian's Allegory of Marriage, The Fortune Teller by Caravaggio – where the light coming down through the frosted skylights gave the room a funny, icy kind of feeling, but in a good way, in a euphoric way. The light was sublime.

At around one in the afternoon we began looking for Raphael's apartment, which was in the 14th arrondissement. We took the four line to Alésia station and within less than a half hour found the address and entered the building and walked up several flights of stairs and knocked on the door. Raphael's mother opened the door and welcomed us warmly and graciously. Raphael beamed when he saw us and he'd invited three of his friends to come as well. We were invited to sit down and Raphael's mother rolled out a cart full of pastries. I helped myself to a macarón with a filling of strawberry jam and thanked her profusely.

Raphael was eager to hear what we thought of Paris and I said I positively loved it. There was so much life, so much variety, so many odd and wonderful things. I wasn't used to having my eyes dazzled by so many things. Cities and towns in the U.S. tended to be more uniform and unadorned.

One of Raphael's friends asked if I'd been influenced by French poetry and I answered yes, quite a bit. Baudelaire, Rimbaud, Mallarmé, Le Comte de Lautréamont had all been seminal influences.

And what of American poetry, another friend asked. What is that like now? We've heard names like Allen Ginsberg and Jack Kerouac and Gary Snyder.

Oh yeah, I answered, they're fantastic poets. The trend since Whitman for many has been an opening of the line, a new approach to language that is intended to discover the genius in language, in the English language, of course, but language in general. The majority of poets still consider the writing of poetry to be a craft, and the materials of language as a medium subject to control, as a roughhewn vernacular to be hammered into golden arabesques by way of metrics and rhyme, but the trend among writers like Ginsberg and Burroughs and Frank O'Hara has been to discover the life and vitality in words when they're – how should I put it? – more naturally and spontaneously given to produce sparks of contrast when the driving force is open to impulse and spontaneity. As Ginsberg phrased it in one of his essays, the "spontaneous irrational juxtaposition of sublimely related fact." The focus is on the sound of words, the vowels and consonants, syllables and phonemes, and how they dance and sparkle on the nerves. It's essential, in these conditions and with this set of intentions, to let go of the ego, the narrower confines of one's subjectivity, and let oneself diffuse into the language, melt into it, find total immersion in it.

Another of Raphael's friends asked if they discarded rhythm.

Oh no, I said, not at all. "Rhythm," said Pound, "is a form cut into time." The poem is a sculpture of sound, a phonemic marble, if you will, or granite. The poet Charles Olson called poetry a "high-energy-construct," an "energy-discharge." What he meant is that the energy that propelled the poet to create a poem should be kept fresh, and the way to accomplish that is through the immediacy of the thing, the life-force energizing it, you allow that to create the form of the poem, and you do that through a process of action, of movement, a chain reaction of phenomenological momentum in which one perception leads immediately and directly to another perception. And this must be achieved intuitively. As soon as you begin to worry about things making sense, the jig is up.

Pardon, *qu'est-ce que c'est jig*...I'm sorry....what is 'jig,' asked Raphael's friend, the one who asked about rhythm.

A 'jig' is a lively dance, I answered, that involves a lot of leaping.

You like poems that leap?

I love poems that leap, I said.

Do you know any French? asked another of Raphael's friends.

Not really, no, I answered, apologetically, and with an acute sense of inadequacy. I've begun taking classes in college, but I haven't progressed very far. I've been mainly concentrating on how to read it. But maybe you can help me out with what some of the things here on the cart that Raphael's mother has so generously supplied. What's this, for instance?

C'est un mille-feuille à la framboise, answered Raphael.

A what ?

A mill-foy, I heard him say.

Mill-foy, I repeated. And it has what in it, exactly?

I'm not sure what you call it in English, red berries that look like a...cluster?....

Oh sure, I said, a raspberry.

Raspberry, he said, and he and his friends laughed.

Yeah, it's a funny word, I said. English is full of silly words. Here's one: borborygmus. It refers to the rumbling or gurgling sounds the stomach makes due to an overabundance of fluid and gas in the intestinal tract. It's a form of onomatopoeia.

Ona....

Onomatopoeia. Another funny word. It refers to words that sound like what they mean. Like cuckoo or sizzle.

Sizzle?

Yeah, like the sound of bacon when it's frying in a pan. I love that sound. I can smell it. Just the idea of bacon triggers my olfactory organs.

Old factory?

Olfatory...it's the organs of the nose? You know, smell?
Smell mainly. It comes from Latin *olfacere*, to smell.

Ah yes, said Raphael, in French it is very similar. We say *les
organs olfactifs*. Odor is very important in French. It's why we have
such wonderful perfumes.

And pastries! I chimed in.

Please, urged Raphael's mother, have some more!

And I did. I put another macarón in my mouth.

Do you know the poet Robert Duncan, asked Michel, the
friend who had asked about rhythm earlier.

Oh sure, I answered, he's a wonderful poet. Very romantic.
He's managed to sound modern while expressing a strong romantic
spirit.

I heard him give a reading in Paris, said Michel.

How was it? Was it good?

Oh yes, it was extremely interesting. He talks a great deal
and is very knowledgeable. He talked a lot about angels.

Angels?

Yes, he said that in the 16th century, and earlier, the church
banned talking to angels. But the poets, being fools, were exempted.
Poets could talk to angels.

Duncan is extremely unique, I said. There's a formality to his
work, a very high, transcendent tone that borders on mysticism. This
is extremely unusual in the realm of modern poetry. His lines are
steeped in musicality.

Muse...*qu'est-ce que c'est ?*

Musicality. They're very lyrical. I think that's very hard to
do. It's difficult to concentrate on lyrical effects without sounding
pretentious, or cloying, and Duncan manages to do that quite well.
The poems feel authentic. And intellectually acute.

Do you write poems, Michel asked Anna.

Me? No, but I enjoy poetry, Anna replied.

Who are some of the contemporary poets in France right
now, I asked

There are quite a few, said Raphael. Anne-Marie Albiach, for
example.

Who ?

Anne-Marie Albiach. She came out with a book recently
called *État.*

Michel Deguy, said Cédric, a young man wearing a blazer with a silver spider pinned to his lapel.

Ah oui, oui, said Raphael. He's a very strong poet. He's published many books. He's a very philosophical poet.

We continued talking for well over an hour and I sensed that Raphael's mother had things she'd like to do so I said that Anna and I should probably get going. Raphael thanked us for coming and gave us his address and we thanked Raphael's mother again and headed back to our hotel in the 5th arrondissement.

*   *   *   *   *

It was Anna's turn to get the flu. She'd probably caught it from me. We were also running low on money. It was obvious our European experiment had failed. Living in Europe would be far more complicated and require resources that were way beyond any capacity I had. It was also becoming increasingly obvious that Anna wasn't happy in our marriage.

Anna wired home for money and we reserved a flight leaving from Heathrow airport in England. We headed England the next day although Anna was very sick. I bought a pack of cigarettes which made Anna extremely angry. That's how low in money we were. I seemed to be living on another planet.

It was at the Gare du Nord that Anna told me she wanted to end our marriage. This news wasn't unexpected, but it put me into a state of quiet despair. There was really nothing I could say that would change her heart and I knew it. Meanwhile, a man kept asking me for money. I tried to make him go away, but he didn't speak English, or pretended not to know English. He was unbelievably persistent. I grew hostile and he finally left us alone.

I hoped that once we got back to the Bay Area that Anna might change her mind and give me another chance.

Which, unbelievably, she did. But winning her back completely was going to be tough.

We got together with Gavin the day after we returned. Gavin's right arm was in a cast. He'd had a bad argument with Martina and in his rage threw a punch at the wall, which broke his arm and left a hole in the wall. For some reason, we all decided to spend the day in San Francisco. We went to the aquarium. I remember looking at a lot of fish and a lot of aquatic plants - moon jellies floating listlessly and hypnotically in a giant cylindrical tank and the easy supple slither of giant Pacific octopuses - wondering how much life was left in my marriage. I had a sinking feeling I'd be joining Gavin soon.

We went to Enrico's in North Beach, a popular sidewalk café, and I noticed Richard Brautigan sitting at one of the tables. I was too shy to get up and introduce myself. A girl of about four or five came around the corner, took a look at all the people sitting at their tables talking and drinking coffee, then turned around and disappeared again. Richard Brautigan was the only one to get up from his table and investigate. He returned quickly, so I assumed the girl had already disappeared entirely from the scene, or had reconnected with a parent. Brautigan's concern and reaction impressed me very much.

I got a job working with a painter. He was a big man from Oklahoma and a fast, solid, hardworking guy. We could knock out a two-bedroom apartment in one day. He told a lot of racist jokes which made me squirm and feel uncomfortable but I didn't say anything. I felt like a coward for keeping quiet, though if I'd asked him to stop telling racist jokes I would've been canned instantly. I should've just gotten canned. I still feel ashamed about that.

The man showed me an apartment building and asked if I thought I could handle painting it on my own. He would pay me a flat amount for the whole job, an amount I've totally forgotten, but I clearly remember believing it would take three maybe four days to paint the building and once I got started it became clear it was going to take far longer, possibly two weeks, which meant I was working for pennies. Unfortunately, I'd also gotten someone else involved, a young man from Bremen, Germany named Dieter Schröder.

Dieter was married to one of Anna's closest friends, Sally Zielinski. We spent a lot time with them. Dieter was an exceptionally handsome man – Anna called him Apollo – and very bright and full of curiosity about things. He was especially passionate about science fiction and – true to the German stereotype – completely in love with technology. Electronic technology in particular, and anything to do with artificial intelligence. He was also quite fascinated by concepts having to do with space and time: deep time, dynamical time, hypertime, imaginary time, polychronicity, time asymmetry, time dilation, warp velocity, wormholes and spacetime foam.

Dieter and I got along quite well and became very close friends. Which is why, when it became apparent that Dieter was looking for work, I offered him the job of painting the apartment building with me. He was quite happy to join me.

It was hard, monotonous work, but we passed the time talking while running our rollers up and down walls applying a coat of desert brown to the stucco walls of the building. A very attractive young woman was leaving her apartment one afternoon and was dressed to the nines in a tight skirt and frilly white blouse. I watched as Dieter focused on the woman and as he leaned to watch as she went around a corner his ladder began sliding from the wall – the roller leaving a downward arcing swath of desert brown as Dieter and his tray of paint spilled to the ground. I found this hilarious and doubled up on the ground from laughing so hard.

We were exhausted at the end of the day and I must've been too tired to clean my tray and brushes. The Oklahoman exploded in rage all over me one morning because I hadn't cleaned things properly. He couldn't fire me because he'd end up having to finish the building himself and pay me fairly for the work we'd done. In order to get paid, we'd have to finish the job. I hated every minute of it. But I felt particularly bad for Dieter. Neither of us were being payed fairly.

Dieter's wife Sally got us work painting offices at a building in downtown San José that had for many years been chiefly a place of medical and dental offices. The rooms had beautiful wood trimming and a few still had dental chairs in them. I enjoyed this work since we were able to listen to music while we worked. Dieter got another job and left me on my own. The job morphed into a more general position of doing repairs and installing lights and working with the building engineer, a seriously neurotic man in his fifties named Hershel. Hershel never smiled, never joked, never enjoyed small talk or showed any interest in me. He just pointed out things that needed doing, gave me a brief lesson on how to best accomplish my task, and went about his business. Whatever was churning inside that man was eating him alive. I was sure that if I accidentally brushed his skin I'd get a shock.

I did not like being back in the United States. I'd forgotten how singularly obsessed everyone was with making money, and how crass and shallow that mindset made everything. I carried France around in me like a dream.

2 Poems

☆

Jesse Glass

The Shower

I shower   run the soap over
belly & cock
& push the soap
over chest &
work it through the
flesh
down the legs
over the wide feet

the suds fall   the soap
breaks in two
in my hand

this is all I have

I sqweege the mirror
with a towel
& the face returns
the upper lip

growing
wires of gray hair
& the pulsing throat
& the hair weeping white water
down throat & back

naked
before the mirror
I am a thing
in the world
participating in its mystery
the belly starting to flab
the cock
pointing to the left foot

I want this body burnt
when it dies   want
to rise in a sunburst like in
some Persian miniature
in which the scimitar
falls
& the blood explodes
from the heart

these hands that
stretch the blue-white
skin
& pull the razor

this is all I have

all that is capable
of casting a shadow
on rented walls
on morning sidewalks
across the empty windows
of the shops

I give to you.

Rubbings

Death's-head gnashes teeth--tells us
Flesh is grass. We
stretch rice paper over his sockets
& rub

his voice with our fists. A
name appears, sharp
and strange.
Dates float through
black wax shavings.
Then

an epitaph climbs beneath
to hang in a web of cracks. We've
traveled

to steal these pictures for our walls: the
weeping willows and maidens minus arms
fascinate us, comfort us,

when life roars loudest they whisper
smallest: *"Here is the zenith*
of night where one star wobbles/
light
knocks on the sheath of the closed
eye that sees

us. Truly, delight man
in no-thing, in
words that dissolve, in
silence between words and pro-
found silence

of clay and the splintered bed
that calls--with the voices
of winterwind and rain--of

hands pointing
to imaginary comforts.
Believe us if you hunger." Surely

we must return
to one limestone angel
fallen in the weeds.

And you do, little one:
weep for the angel
who stares at nothing.

from Glyphmachine

☆

Lily Robert-Foley

The following is an extract from the unpublished novel
Glyphmachine, *set in a universe oddly dissimilar to our own where*
climate change acceleration has forced the mainstream to the brink
with shrinking resources, the ever widening chasm between rich and
poor, and a privately owned government operating as a totalitarian
police state. Our main character, Brune, has crossed the border from
California into Mexico looking for her missing sister Clara, and along
her journey finds herself in the Pluriversidad, *an occupied University*
campus in Vera Cruz, and one of the many expressions of the
resistance movements that populate the world of Glyphmachine.

17.

Brune was entirely alone apart from one snoring mass at
the far end of the room. Her implants read 8pm. She had slept six
straight hours. She scrambled to sit up, checking to make sure her
bag was still there, although there was nothing particularly valuable
in it. Still. She didn't know these people. She smelled like old
cheese, and she desperately had to pee.

It looked as though everyone else had simply left their

bedding where it lay in piles all across the expanse of room-spanning collective mattress. And so she did the same. She strapped on her bag and put on her shoes this time at the exit so as not to sully the soft floor intended for sleepers. Thankfully, she easily found a door reading *baño* a few steps down the hallway to her right, though as she stepped inside she found herself at a loss to reconcile it with any prior notion she could have had of a bathroom. The room itself was a mishmash of cracked concrete slab and earth, as though someone had tried to rip up a concrete floor but abandoned their work partway through. Along the far wall, a thin makeshift bench, almost more like a flat railing, ran at knee height from one end of the room to the other. Three long sheets were attached to hoops hanging from a track set into the ceiling. As she approached the far end of the room she could see that deep holes had been dug into the ground. There was a faint, but very faint odor of piss and shit as she stood over one and looked down into its putrescent bowels.

After a moment of confusion and hesitation, Brune pulled one of the circle canopy sheets over to her from a few feet away along the track, and arranged it around herself with the hole in the center. She felt precious within the canopy, as though inside an egg. She pulled down her pants and settled her thighs onto the thin bench, leaving her privates to hang off behind her over the hole. She released a long stream of warm piss that resounded deep below like someone running the tap in the apartment next door. She finished and only then, thankfully noticed two nozzles attached to tubes running from the wall, hanging on little claws next to her. She unhooked one and pressed a little button under the nozzle and got a powerful blast of warm air full on in the face. She was more careful as she took the next one, pointing it away from her as it emitted a blossom spray of water. She rinsed and dried herself with the two nozzles, and by the time she had her pants up and was ready to leave, she had begun to wonder how something so intricately abstruse and unnecessary as the porcelain toilet had ever come into existence. At what point did people start believing that a toilet had to be anything more complicated than a hole in the ground?

Luckily the hallway leading back to the staircase went in a straight line. She could hardly imagine what terrors or wonders awaited in getting lost amid the daunting fun house of intricate machines on either side.

She emerged into the courtyard to find sets of people seated on chairs and pillows on the ground in intersecting circles, while another formed a cluster around a table from which an enticing smell emanated. She stood for a moment not sure what to do, until the roaring emptiness of her stomach directed her. The small cluster parted organically for her, letting her through to a table spread with a platter of tamales, a huge pot of millet, a pot of beans, an iridescent algae based salsa, a foot-high stack of light blue tortillas, and some odd white items in a bowl, the color and texture of peeled hardboiled eggs, yet shaped like starfish. Brune paused in front of them, trying to place the objects into a pre-existing category.

Next to her stood an astonishingly beautiful young man who was naked except for a confounding assembly of mismatched fabrics round his waist, and sashes and chains hung round his neck. He was barefoot. Brune mused involuntarily upon how the garment stayed up and how easy it would be to take off. He swung a curtain of long dark brown hair over his shoulder to reveal an evocative profile and turned to look at Brune. His eyes were a very light brown and shimmered like tiger-stone.

"3D printed gelatin starfish eggs," he said, looking Brune directly in the eye.

Brune could not speak, lost as she was hesitating between whether the strangeness of his eyes, their liquid attraction, stemmed from him or from her.

"Beautiful, no?" he continued, holding one in his hand and biting off the top arm of the star.

Brune, still struggling, managed a yes.

"And tasty too," he said. Brune watched him chew and swallow, remarking abnormally pointed incisors, and the gentle slip of a muscle under his jaw that moved just a little with every chew. "I haven't seen you around here before. I'm Xbalanqué."

"Guh?"

"Xbalanqué. I'm named after one of the twins from the *Popul Vuh*. My parents were born in Germany so I could have been a Hans or a Dieter I suppose, but they are descendants." He gestured towards a circle of people on the far side of the room, and Brune assumed his parents were among them. Descendants? "But I was born here, a child of the Pluriversidad."

He put a starfish on her plate.

Brune was not sure she was ready for all this friendliness, nor if she was prepared to be inadvertently seduced by a teenage hippie super model. On top of everything else, she felt distinctly like she was coming down off a three-month long benzo addiction. Because she was. But she was in no position to take counter action, so she followed suite.

"Brune. I'm, I'm new here. Lupe and Maria brought me."

He spooned some algae salsa on top of the millet and beans on Brune's tortilla. "Home grown *alga*," he said. "Come." His smile embodied goof mixed with unwitting elegance. He then picked up a small round dried gourd from a collection at the end of the table and poured something from a larger gourd into it and handed it to her. Brune peered inside. It looked like water sprinkled with tiny flecks of something like shiny fish food.

"Sea monkeys."

"What?"

"They purify the water, as well as aid in hydration absorption. It's part of a fertilizer system we use for the plants, but turns out it gets humans just a little bit high. And it's pretty tasty. You'll like it, everyone does. It's subtle."

Brune swirled her cup around trying to decipher if the 'sea monkeys' were alive, and wondering if everything at the Pluriversidad was designed to get its inhabitants high. Not to say that didn't seem like a wholeheartedly worthy goal. She took a sip. It tasted like a delicate floral lemonade that had sprung from a deep underground well and was slightly effervescent. She took another sip. A light caress smoothed the hard surface of her benzo comedown, ever so slightly.

Brune followed Xbalanqué to a circle of people on the opposite side of the room from where his parents presumably were. He sat down on a long mat woven from multicolored recycled plastics, in-between the legs of a tall woman with silver hair who was also naked to the waist, wearing what looked like Trumppolice© pants. Her head was propped up on the lap of a plump middle-aged woman with un unkempt afro who had finished her food and was now braiding the Trumppolice© pants woman's hair. A gender indeterminate person wearing face paint and a gold shorts jumpsuit was delicately plucking a stringed instrument that looked like a mix between a Kalimba and a Guzheng but with a series of dials, tubes, and what appeared to be whammy bars on one end. The music wove rhythmically and unobtrusively into their conversation like an ivory inlay. The silver haired woman wore a half smile, and spoke through long, elegant eyes. Brune sat on the floor at the edge of the mat near Xbalanqué (whose name she had completely forgotten). The group included four other people whose limbs splayed dynamically and interlacing on sewn cushions and mats, and one on a little wooden stool. They engaged in chaotic languaging as tongues flowed freely from one to the other, bathed in a shower of dissenting opinion. Deciphering the English was task enough for Brune, and as she did so, she had the impression she was listening to a page from a transcript torn in two.

"The *form* preserves the hierarchy, and so the person embodies the reproduction of that structure whether they aim to or not."

"I'm not sure her point is to alter the paradigm."

"The bibliography has no reflection on the politics of citationality."

"There can be more than one way of doing research."

"Maybe there was, maybe there wasn't."

"Obviously, but is it relevant, *that's* my question."

"Does science precede magic or does magic precede science?"

"Sure, but so what?"

"It's the old question of strategy, there are and must be multiple strategies of resistance for a movement to succeed."

"It's the snake eating its own tail."

"No, it's more about conflicting yet complementary patterns of change. Like the book, old technologies do not necessarily die because new technologies are born."

"Or the Klein bottle."

"Are you sure she's for the movement?"

"If you do not politicize your research, it will be politicized by default."

"It was totally inflated with Westnorthern epistemology."

"Or a Mobius strip."

"Where do you think your rhetoric comes from?"

"The book is a terrible example."

"Where do you think the apparatus of rhetoric comes from

period?"

"Lectures are *boring*."

"Learning happens in social encounters."

"I want to use exclusively Southern epistemologies."

"Are we not interacting socially now?"

"But what is the role of the teacher then?"

"Don't you hear how absurd you sound using the word epistemology in this context?"

"Doesn't that just repeat the same cycle?"

"You can do whatever you want."

"Raw material?"

"I was just saying that she's *just* a researcher. She's not a revolutionary."

"I disagree, I think she is a revolutionary. What she's saying is completely revolutionary."

"How so?"

"Can content alone be revolutionary?"

"Spluh, but it's not enough to change the paradigm."

"Content and form are not opposed."

"Content doesn't exist."

"Form doesn't exist."

"Yes they are."

"It's a contradiction."

"Good!"

"I mean, is it conscious."

"I say down with intellectual monuments, we don't need them to carry out our research."

"Does it need to be?"

"And can she plant a tomato."

"That truly is the question."

"To the tomato!"

"To mato!"

They all raised their small gourds up and repeated "To mato!" dissolving into laughter and smaller conversation splinters. Brune looked around helplessly for Lupe and Maria, and finally caught sight of Lupe's feathered neck three circles over. She and Maria seemed to be passionately entrenched in a conversation with an older woman sitting on a chair and wearing a tiny pillbox hat decorated with colored paper and shells. Brune felt sheepish, and looked to Xbalanqué for help, but he seemed to be very distracted nestling his face into the silver haired woman's inner thigh. Plus, Brune still could not remember his name. She contented herself to concentrating on her food while trying to recede into the background. Xbalanqué hadn't been lying about the food. Brune had not tasted a fresh egg since she was a teenager, and she became almost emotional as she rolled bites of the starfish around in her mouth. She let herself wander passively through the melodic patterns of the instrument and the conversation, her vision wandering from face to face around the room.

"It can be intimidating at first," a light, fragile voice spoke up next to her. "But it's not on purpose." Brune turned to face the soft voice that had almost instantaneously put her at ease. Intimidating, perhaps, but certainly not unwelcoming. The voice belonged to a small person, perhaps a man half in and half out of drag, or a woman, half in and half out of drag, or both, or neither. They had sleek black hair shaved along the sides, the top tied back in a pony tail, and their dark-skinned face had been contoured with makeup, but left partially undone, like a half hung gallery exhibition. They had black eyes like outer space, that seemed almost taken aback by their own enigma, and drew Brune to them like a journey to an unknown destination.

"I'm Marca," the person said holding out their fingers in the five fingered web Brune had seen Maria and Lupe make.

"Brune," she said looking uneasily at the fingers.

"You press your fingertips to mine," Marca said, sweetly, and Brune did so.

"Thanks. It's been a long journey" Brune said, as though that explained something.

Marca did not ask where from. And in spite of the fact that they had started the conversation, they seemed almost embarrassed to continue it. This gave Brune confidence, as other people's awkwardness can when not muted by shame. Marca played with the strings of a robe made from what looked like burlap tied in a sash across the front. They somehow cast Brune in the opposite social role from the one she had just occupied, and Brune found herself agreeably inspired to lead the conversation forward.

"Have you ever met anyone named Roxana?" Brune asked.

"Roxana? Long black hair, round face, possibly insane?"

Brune nodded.

"That's her."

"Yes, why?"

"She... she looks a lot like my sister."

"Oh."

"Like, exactly like my sister."

"That's weird."

"Crazy weird."

"Sometimes that happens," said Marca.

"Yes but, not like this. I mean, it's uncanny. Like, maybe they could be the same person."

Marca nodded thoughtfully and didn't say anything, and yet silence has textures, and Marca's silence was a breathable kind, full of porous holes and openings, like a welcoming curtain flapping in a breeze to reveal glimpses of a mountain nestled village behind. It did not shut her down, it made her want to speak. Brune went on:

"The thing is, Clara–that's my sister. She went to Mexico about six weeks ago, and at first she was writing me emails all the time and then she just stopped responding. It's not like her. She always responds to me. Sometimes it takes a few days but, she always responds. That's why I came to Mexico, to look for her. But then I lost my bag at the bus station in Mexico City. And Maria and Lupe found me and brought me here."

"Would your sister have any reason to want to hide her identity? Sometimes people at the Pluriversidades are engaged in not so legal activities."

"Maybe... she was secretive. Is." [...]

The musical accompaniment that had peppered the discussion when Brune arrived had grown progressively more complex as other instruments joined in one by one around the courtyard, at odd intervals. A tall man with aqua colored dreadlocks had started banging on a drum a few meters away, while smaller people–his children perhaps–joined him on percussive objects of all orders, from a small thumb piano to the back of a pot. Someone stood in the corner with a flute of many tubes fashioned out of pipes and horns of different metals. Xbalanqué had wandered off at some point to join a group of people pushing and pumping the largest accordion Brune had ever seen, that appeared to be filtered and amplified via a cord attached to a dainty upright switchboard. Two people in bird costumes held aloft a rack attached with strings while people danced about underneath plucking in a seemingly random arrangement, yet producing something that resonated at an odd harmony with the diverse sounds coming from around the room. Some bodies had simply started singing or chanting or even reading poems off of their implants. An old man with a giant exposed potbelly was projecting a visual poem above them in a cloud that alternated in pulsing arabesques between different alphabets, appearing and disappearing in an elegant choreography. It was chaos and cacophony yet somehow it came together in a harmonious ecology. Brune imagined the progressive formation of social infrastructures patterned and modulating in viral flows across geographies in allegory to the music surrounding her.

The view out the open side of the courtyard had grown progressively darker while sunlight faded into night. This produced an odd effect on the underside of the solar panels that swirled in perpetually dazzling patterns above them. Although the lights did seem to grow darker, they did not fade completely, they more so shifted, into darker, lush hues, like the aurora borealis. The hues fell across the faces and bodies of the Pluriversidad inhabitants, painting them in undulating color elegies. Elegies as energies seemed to both subdue and to enliven the bodies, as they peeled off one by one from their dining circles to dance and sing, dropping their plates, bowls and cups in a basin on the table where leftovers of the food still remained. Only a few stray souls remained in intimate diminuendo to speak softly underneath the quilt of music and chanting. Even Marca had been drawn off, her hand clasped by a passing dancer, caught by the trail of a beat, into the nebulous circle of people dancing amidst the instruments.

Brune felt at once abandoned and married into the swarm. She felt the beat of her blood through her heart whisper out to her core and limbs to move with the sounds, move with the others. But Brune was not a dancer. She had been too trained in the ugliness of her body as perceived by her fantasy of others' gazes, and had not learned to hear the beauty of her body that lived in the sophisticated wisdom of her organs and viscera, blood, bone and skin. Brune's comfort zone was a lost galaxy, and she hovered light years from it, suspended in an alien satellite off a moon whose color she could not name. Time became ethereal and unquantifiable, both momentary and interminable as she sunk into a trance-like state where boredom and fascination met. The dance and music were hypnotic.

After several or hundreds of minutes, a small discreet figure came and sat next to her.

"A little too much?"

It was Marca, whose body she had witnessed in flecks among the miasma of skin, fabric and instruments. Brune nodded.

"I don't really understand where I am."

Marca laughed. A laugh, full hearted yet demure, like a distant bird song.

"I think that's maybe a good place to start."

They sat and watched without saying anything.

"Are you guys preparing a show or something?"

"We don't call it a show; we call it a Rumble." [...]

Brune was not a musical expert but she had taken seven years of piano lessons at her mother's uncontestable behest from ages six to thirteen. She could identify no central argument to the arrangement, which she assumed was improvised. There was no guiding drum beat or bass line, no familiar scale or chord pattern to hold on to. The music seemed as though it were a collection of utterly unconnected conversations, more like listening to a crowded bar than a musical performance. An aviary. A conference of the birds. [...]

They sat in the sound surrounded silence for several long moments until Brune, needing a break, asked if there was a place she could take a shower. Marca indicated that there was, in the basement of the East wing, in an equivalent position to where the bedroom was on the West, and pointed to the opposite side of the large shaped U building that framed the interior courtyard. Brune thanked her, stood, and made her way through the titillated crowd and down into the East Wing's belly.

At the end of the basement hallway, Brune found a large room roughly the same dimensions as the bedroom she had slept in that afternoon. The room looked like an underwater grotto that had been lovingly decorated by baroque mermaids with a lot of time on their hands. Although bits of what must have been the original concrete wall still remained, the vast majority of it had been painstakingly tiled in the most whimsical mosaics Brune had ever seen. She remained agape several instants, but she could not help walking slowly around the room following the walls, which were a mix of abstract patterns, arabesques, geometric shapes and lines interspersed with figural depictions that were largely animal themed. Human beings were portrayed staggered among oversized big cats, birds and reptiles, all of whom were shown engaging in different activities together: eating, sleeping, dancing, lovemaking (?) weaving tapestries, sculpting, holding congress, writing, playing music on instruments, some of them similar to those she had seen in the courtyard. In certain depictions, the animals and humans seemed to be working together at odd interfaces with buttons, dials and screens, or sorting and connecting colorful cables between machines some of which Brune vaguely recognized from her passage through the basement hallway. The tiles themselves seemed to be made out of anything its creators could have gotten their hands on: bits of glass and shells, chips of different colored plastics, bottle caps, buttons, keyboard letters, tokens, old coins from defunct currencies, screws, bolts, nails, rocks, wires....

Brune paused at the back wall, deciphering what looked like big ships arriving over a sea and white faced men in colonial wear pouring off boats with lances and swords. And then, at the corner where one wall met another, it showed the large birds flying off into a starry night sky, and a series of violent eruptions of abstract streaks and shapes in bright colors as though the reptiles, cats and humans were erupting into strange clouds scattered into the earth and sky. As Brune paused momentarily to try to see if she could make out an image or a story within the abstraction, the ceiling above her opened and a fine volley of water drops poured down on top of her head. Before she could think to step to the side, she was drenched head to toe, her synthetic fibers sticking to her like a plastic bag flung against a wall in a storm. She ran back to the doorway to seek cover, noticing as she got there the trail of shoe prints she had made across the room. The shower remained contained in a single cylinder at the other end of the room where Brune had stood a moment ago, while the rest of the room remained dry.

This was the shower room then.

There were no stalls.

Brune was philosophically averse to getting naked in any place where she might be witnessed by more than one person at a time. She had never had the classic college threesome, and was part of that stubborn fringe group that insists on wearing bathing suits in the sauna. For the first two or three years of her sex life (which didn't officially begin until she was 23, FYI), she tried for the most part to keep her shirt on during sex. She remembered a very hot and uncomfortable afternoon on a naked beach in Martinique with Clara, fixing her eyes obsessively on the horizon in order to avoid catching glimpses of the drooping pot bellies and curdled buttocks of the elderly, or at the firm chiseled bodies of the young gay men, or of Clara's dizzyingly plump breasts.

She stood like a wet puppy for a moment in the entryway trying to decide what to do. She resolved finally, as there was no one else in the room, to try to take the fastest shower of her life. She laid her clothes and shoes on the shelf by the door where she also found a basin full of light green balls wrapped in cheesecloth-like netting affixed with a string you could wear around your neck, that she assumed were soap. There was also a folded stack of thin porous material that she concluded was towels. The ceiling seemed dotted all the way across with little openings for the water to come out, and was apparently activated by a motion censor (did this mean it was cleaned in the nude?). She thus stuck as close as she could to the wall closest the door, and closest the shelf with her clothes on it.

She stood for a moment, her bare skin feeling like the top of a mountain, struggling to reconcile the feeling of reckless exposed abandon with her body shame. But as the water came down over her, she could see and feel her skin being lit up with the same sea monkeys that had been in her drinking water earlier. Their entire stock of water must have been continuously purified and recycled with them. She closed her eyes and allowed the water to wash away the journey. And as it did so, before she could stop it, it began to go deeper, to wash deeper, to begin to strip away paths of sadness set into the layers of her skin. Her failed dissertation, the symbolic violence of the University, Hélène's suicide and the rehabilitation center, the attitude of her so-called friends during the whole fiasco, and deeper still, her jealousy of Ninon, her mother's disappointment, her father's disinterest, her passionate longing to find Clara, to be Clara. She rubbed her hands over the soap and through her hair, the healing touch of her own fingers spreading deep into her neural pathways like the root tendrils of a plant.

Her reverie was abruptly interrupted by an intersecting sprinkler set of giggles penetrating the doorway. Her eyes shot open to witness three women flinging off their clothes in elastic haste, and throwing them in a disordered fashion onto the shelf where Brune had laid her clothes in a bundle. They ran chasing each other like ecstatic guppies, forming a circle holding hands in the center of the room. They were singing in a disorganized round, frighteningly erotic harmonies. When one left one harmony off, another caught it up, improvising arpeggio and aria as the water began to fall over them. They broke the circle and melded together becoming the appendages of a many limbed goddess. They ran their hands across one another's skins and through one another's hair, kissing each other ravenously, tenderly on the mouth, on the neck, between the breasts, down the belly, until one reached the center of another's hearth stone nectar, on her knees, burying her face deep into her pudenda. The two who remained standing drank from one another's tongues, rubbing their hands languorously over one another's breasts, backs, thighs and buttocks. They were a sensuous, malleable sculpture of organic tissues, and Brune could not tear her eyes away in spite of a suffocating grease layer of shame coating her. She fought against the violent licks of desire that flared up through her belly. A few moments were almost enough to send her doubling up in orgasm, if only she could touch herself, yet she held herself back, together, held herself in. She turned around putting her back between herself and them, washing as quickly as she could her underarms, her face, her feet. She knew from the smell, from the sticky discomfort that had begun to accompany her already on the long bus ride from the border that she had to wash her vagina. Yet she could not bring herself to. She left it alone to fester in untouched solitude. She stepped out from under the nebulous drops, grabbed a towel and her wet clothes and quickly found herself dripping in the hallway, wrapped in a nearly see-through hand-woven towel carrying a pile of still sopping wet clothes, helplessly wondering what the hell to do next. As nothing logical revealed itself to her, she burst into tears.

If interested in reading the whole novel, please contact lilyrobertfoley@gmail.com

Selections from the upcoming novel
An Evening of Romantic Lovemaking

☆

Ben Slotky

Jellybeans and Orgies

Folks, thank you very much for that smattering of applause. That's, yeah, that's a very adequate amount, it's accurate, it is. For what you're about to receive. [Smirks, smiles, paces. Holding microphone with right hand, pointing out to crowd with left]. My name is Ben Slotky, and a little bit about me. I am forty-five years old. [Tilts head at crowd]. I know, I know. I look great, thank you, ma'am. That is a preemptive thank you. Like you don't even have to *say* it, you know? It's like I know you that well already. It's amazing, isn't it? How good I look, and I'm forty-five, I'm *married*, I have six kids.
Yeah.
I do.
I have six, six boys. Oldest is 17, youngest are twins, they're two. Two years old, ma'am, is what those two are right there. How about it, right? [Looks knowingly at crowd, nods head] We'll get into it, we will, but a little bit about *me*, I live in Bloomington. That's right, right here. I *do* own this place, this place right here. That's right. [Holds hands out. Looks up and around] Built it, renovated it, did all that, did all this. So, I did this, built this. [Stops mid-stride.Pause. Looks

out. No applause]. Huh. Kind of thought there'd be something there.
A clap, a woo-hoo. But nothing? That's about right, that's about
right. [Continues pacing, head down] I live in Bloomington, I work
here in Bloomington, and a little bit about *me*? Like one thing I *do*?
Like if somebody tells me they're from a city. Like I ask and they say
they're from Cincinnati. [Looks into crowd] Like ma'am, say you're
from Cincinnati. Like I'll go where're you from and you go I'm from
Cincinnati.

Where're you from, ma'am?

[Looks out, eyes wide. Pauses. Nods head.]

Oh really? How many people live there? *That's the first thing I'll
say!* Every time! I don't know why. I'm very interested in how many
people live in places. [Looks up toward ceiling. Quizzical look on
face.]

Oh, you're from Des Moines? How many people live there?

[Looks back at crowd]

And what am I going to do with that, you know? Like what am I
going to do with how many people live in Des Moines? Why is this
so important, ma'am? Why is this the first thing, always the first
thing? But I can't not do it, I can't. [Pacing] Like I don't care what you
do, for a living, I don't, I don't care, but for some reason, I want to
know how many people live in a town. So that's a little bit about me.
Something else about me is, [scratches head, rubs stomach] what
else, what else? [Looks out at crowd] Because I feel as if we should,
you know, get to know each other better, right? Circumstances being
what they are and all?

So you know how sometimes there's a jar of jellybeans? You know
how sometimes there's a [Pauses, looks intently at audience]
ma'am, you know!

You've seen *jars*, right?

You're familiar with jars.

You know what a jelly bean is. So imagine if you will a jar full of jelly
beans, like imagine it. [Clasps hands together, tilts head, wide-eyed
look of wonder] Just *imagine* it! [Looks back out at crowd, crouches
down, looks conspiratoraly side to side] That was a quick impression
right there, that was me doing a guy who was really excited about
the prospect of imagining a jar full of jellybeans, folks. That's what
that was. To clarify. [Blinks quickly, stands back up, continues
pacing] A jar full of jellybeans and we're all imagining it, right? We

see it, we've got it, and then imagine somebody comes up to me and goes, "Hey Ben, how many jellybeans do you think are in that jar?" And I'd go "I don't know, I don't know" or something like that. And they'd go "Do you think there's like *sixty-five jellybeans* in that jar?" And I'd look and go "Yeah, about sixty-five jellybeans, that sounds about right." You know I'd look at the jar, I'd gauge it, right? I'd do some jellybean-gauging, some jar-gauging and I'd be like "Ok, yeah, about sixty-five, about sixty five." [Nods head up and down assuredly] And then they'd say something like "Or do you think there's like *seven hundred and fifty jelly beans* in there? Does that sound right?" And I'd pause and I'd look again and I'd go "Yeah.... yeah, there's probably about seven hundred and fifty of them." You know, so that's a little bit about me, is that I'm not a good judge about how many jellybeans would be in a jar, what else? Uh, a little bit about *me*, I don't know if I'm an *orgy guy*. [Quick, embarrassed scrunch of face, quick shake of head] You know what I mean, I mean I don't think I'm a, I don't know if I'm an *orgy guy*. And by that I mean, and let me clarify, by that I mean I don't know if I would participate in an orgy. You know what I mean? I just don't think I'd do it, and I've been thinking about this a while, if I was an orgy guy or not, because I *assumed* that I was, you know what I mean? [Looks out at crowd] Fellas? You know this, right? What I mean? Like if somebody were to say "hey, would you like to go *into* an orgy?" Like theoretically, a hypothetical orgy. [Pauses. Laughs] And you know, me saying that somebody would say "would you like to go into an orgy," like that's how that would go, that's the way you'd get invited to an orgy, that kind of shows how not an orgy guy I am, doesn't it? "Say fella, how's about going into this swell orgy, we've got here!" Anyway, but no, seriously, let's say I'm invited to a hypothetical orgy, would I go? And I'd like to think I'd be like "Yeah, I'll go," you know? Like I'd think about it, I'd ruminate for a second. I'd consider it, I'd gauge, I'd orgy-gauge, [Pauses, confused and amused look on face]and there's been a lot of gauging already, hasn't there? By my count, it's like two types of gauging, jellybean and orgy, and what this has to do with an evening of romantic lovemaking I have yet to determine, but we'll have to muddle through, I guess, but anyway, yeah, like *previously*? Previously, I'd be like yeah, I'll go to the orgy, you know, but now I think no, no way, you know? No way would I go, nothing about it sounds good to me. I don't think I'd do that, go to an orgy. And that's a big deal, you know? Because you go through life and you think something is one thing and then it turns out to be another thing. You know how that is? [Pauses, shakes head. Squints eyes and squeezes bridge of nose. Exhales loudly.] And I know, and I know how this sounds, it sounds silly. You're like oh, this is jellybeans and orgies, that's what this is. A goof, a lark. A hoo-haw. [Looks mock-sternly out at crowd]

Ma'am, are you here thinking this is a hoo-haw? Like a good old-fashioned hoo-haw? I can't see you out there, so I'm assuming. I'm surmising, and while I'm doing that, I want to assure you that this isn't. This is serious. This is a declaration. I am declaring, confessing, here. These are things I am sharing, little bits of things. Jellybean things, orgy things.

I am explaining how all of these things lead up to this thing. The hostage thing, the doors-are-locked thing. The imminent foreclosure thing.

This is a narrative progression, ma'am. A through-line, if you will, a discernible plot, so *that's* a little bit about me, so that's good, we're sharing. And what else, what else. I stopped masturbating. [Pauses]. Thank you, I miss it, I do, I miss masturbating. I think about it, you know? I think about picking it back up, and by "it" I mean the act of masturbating, not my wiener, right? I don't mean that. I mean, I'm not standing up here in front of you good people talking about picking up my wiener, am I? No way, that's gross, it's *gross*. Save that kind of talk for the orgy guys, is what I say. But, no seriously, I think the thing I miss most about masturbating, and I've thought about this, I have. Like a lot. People always ask me, they're like "What do you miss most about masturbating," and by "people" I mean "nobody," and by "a lot" I mean "none ever." Like that's never happened, nobody's ever said to me "what do you miss most about masturbating." That's not like a phrase anybody's ever said, I don't think, to me. Like I'm not saying it's never happened, ma'am, you know?

Never say nobody's never said what do you miss most about masturbating, you know that old adage?

That old saying?

That old chestnut? That old Brazil nut?

No, nobody's ever said that, I don't think. *I've* never said, that's for sure, but you know what I *did* say the other day? I said, uh, to my

wife I said "next time you're making *quinoa*...?"
[Pauses. Laughs quickly].
That's what I said, I said "next time you're making *quinoa*..?" Like
that, like a question, voice trailing off and all that. And I stopped
myself, you know? Because how was that going to end, you know?
That sentence, that request. Seems innocuous, seems benign, but
it wasn't, and you know what? It's because right then I realized I
wasn't an orgy guy. No orgy guy would say that, would he? To his
wife? Next time you're making *quinoa*? And I'll be honest, I didn't
even finish that sentence, not then, so I'm not going to finish this, I
don't think. We've got a lot to get to tonight folks.
We're just getting started.

The Kind of Chicken I Like

[Looks around, pauses, starts again.] I'd know if I was retarded,
right? Like I'd know, by now? I mean, I'm almost fifty years old, and
by almost fifty, I mean forty-five. Two score and five. That's how old I
am, and you'd think that by now I'd know if I was retarded, right?
Were retarded? Asking, blinking. Wide-eyed. You'd think that
would've come up. Like it would have been mentioned, and I'm
asking this only because I feel like I say things a retarded person
would say, and by that I mean I say things I think a *mentally* retarded
person would say. My friend Jordan's physically retarded. This isn't
that, that's not what I'm saying I'm not saying I'm saying things a
physically retarded person would say, and I know, and I know.
You can't say retarded.
Not anymore you can't. You can't, you just can't say it.
Used be, he said, hitching up pants.
Time was, he said, squinting into the distance.
I reckon a man used'ta be able to say retarded all day, were he so
inclined, I do declare. But now? Now you *can't* say it and I don't
mean you, ma'am. Not you in particular, ma'am. I'm not saying *you*
can't say it. You can say retarded, I'm guessing, probably, right?
You have that ability, right? Of course you can. You can and you're
allowed to. You can say whatever you want. This is America. This
is land of free, this is home of brave. That sounds like an Indian,
doesn't it? A Native Indian. A Native Indian-American. Home of
Brave. One time when I was a kid, I made this joke. I was like 7

or 8. I said "what state's Dolly Parton from?" And the answer was "Massive Two-tits." That's instead of Massachusetts, ma'am.

In case you were.

Lest there be.

On the off chance that.

Google hemming, google hawing.

And that was a joke and I told that, and this was then, all of this was. So then. Then AF, as the kids say, and by kids, I mean my kids. They say AF, which stands for as fuck. It's cute. I say it too, except I say it wrong. I say school AF and breakfast AF. I do that on purpose. We have a lot of fun, my kids and I do, and that's maybe not the point, unless it is. If that's not the point, then the point is this, and that is that I think I'd know if I was retarded. I'm fairly sure about this, pretty sure about this. I used to think I was dead. It's possible, I guess, and would make more sense, and I get it, this is starting not to make sense.

This is wheeling, this is veering.

Careening.

Let me explain. Here is something I said. I said this, said all of this, and I need you to tell me if this sounds like something a not-retarded person would say.

A popular misconception, and I'm going to get this out there, I'm going to get this out, is that I am the heir to the "Shawls, Y'all" fortune.

Let me repeat this. I am not , I'm not the heir to the "Shawls, Y'all" fortune. I don't have anything to do with "Shawls, Y'all." This is not my family's invention, I don't come from "Shawls, Y'all" money, is what I'm saying. This is not true, not true, and this is how this part starts, ma'am. Just like this, just exactly like this, walking, walking. And yeah, and no, and I can say this with almost a hundred percent certainty, about the shawls. Now let's make a couple things clear, and by couple I mean two or more.

One.

I'm not saying there's no chance that I'm not the heir to this fortune. It's not impossible, ma'am. Not beyond the realm, but if I am? If I am, then we're going to have to assume a couple of things, so bear with me. The whole argument that I'm the heir to the "Shawls, Y'all" fortune is predicated on two pretty serious assumptions. One is that my family is somehow affiliated with "Shawls, Y'all", the franchise that's dominated the shawl market of the Southeastern United States for decades. We're going to have to assume that, but before that, and I'm going to ask you seriously here, if you're going to buy a shawl and you're below the Mason/Dixon line, there's pretty much one place you're going to go, isn't there?

You're not going to go to "Yankee Shawls."

You're not going to go to "Lou Rawls' Shawls."

You're not, I'm not, and you're not. You're going to go to "Shawls, Y'all" and that's fine, that's fine, and not what this is about. I mean, we've established that but so what, move on, let's go. So anyway, so shawls, so the notion that I'm the heir to this throne, the Shawls, Y'all throne assumes that my family has something to do with that, and I'm not saying that they didn't, but I, and I can't stress this enough, I don't think, I can't say that they have had anything to do with this, so I really don't feel comfortable saying anything about this at all. That's the first assumption, that's the first.

The second assumption that this notion is predicated upon is that there is such a thing called "Shawls, Y'all;" I don't know if there is, I've never heard of it. Like I don't know that that's even a thing. Shawls, Y'all? Seems like something, right? I mean, it could be a thing, but as far as I know, it isn't. I mean, I've never heard of it, but I don't live in the South. So, there's that, I mean I don't know, maybe? Is it a thing? Probably. I don't know, and again, and you're right, probably is a strong word. Probably is a strong word, ma'am. I don't want to say there probably is such a thing as a store called "Shawls, Y'all," but there could be, I don't know.

My aunt works at a place called Belks or Delks; I've never heard of that, but that's a real thing, I've just never heard of it. I mean, I have heard of it, but I hadn't heard of it until she mentioned it to me. She's going in for tests this week and she may die. She said if she dies, like if she finds out she's going to die, she's going to start getting high and drinking all the time. She's about 80. I think that's OK, you know? So I call her every day and I'm not saying I'm hoping that she dies, but I'd get high and drink, you know? With her, I mean. Or without her. Because of her. Solidarity, is what I'm saying, ma'am. Solidarity, y'all. I wrote a story about my aunt once called 27 Cats. It's nice. It is warm and comforting, not unlike a warm shawl, not unlike a warm segue.

So back to this popular misconception about me and my family owning "Shawls, Y'all". I don't even think it's fair to say that it's a popular misconception, because I'm not sure that it's popular. And by that I mean, I'm not sure anyone's ever said that but me, but I'm saying it, I'm saying it now, just like I was saying it this morning when I was lying in bed this morning, when I'd just woken up, and this is the first thing that is going through my mind, right as I'm waking up, this was, that was, the shawls was, and that's not true because the first thing I was thinking about was a chicken. You ever do that, ma'am? You ever think about a chicken? You know how you're sometimes chicken-thinking? A little pre-dawn, chick-think? That's what this was, this was that. So I'm thinking about what kind of chicken I would eat. The first thing I am thinking about lying in bed this morning is the kind of chicken I will eat, the only kind of chicken I will eat, and I know, and I know. "The first thing?" That was you, ma'am, that was what you were saying, right? That's what you were like? You were like "The *first* thing? Not the hostage taking, the blowing up, the barricading? Not this?" And you're waving your arms around? A'wavin' and a'flailin'? No, and see, and right there, that is what I'm talking about. Maybe I'm not doing a good enough job. It's not about this [waves arms, flails], not about *any* of this. Not about the lights, the marquee, the restoring. It's not about any of that, ever has been, and I am explaining this now, about how there's like one kind of chicken I will eat, and the kind of chicken I will eat has to be raised under some very specific conditions. And it's not, it isn't cage-free, or free-range, I don't think? Not that, ma'am, not free-cage or range-cage? Not that.

Cage rage?

And I'm asking?

And I'm looking up now?

And maybe scratching my head and going huh or hmm? Ma'am? I'm not, and this is important, I'm not a picky eater, I'm not finicky, I'll eat just about anything. Anything except black licorice, and no, and stop. And shot of me shaking head and outstretching hands. Not "anything but black licorice" because of blacks, because of racist. Not that, not that, come on, grow up. I'm clarifying here, establishing. I'm putting in context, I'm framing. I'm saying I'm not picky, I'm saying I'm not racist. I'm saying this is the type of chicken I like, you understand, like to eat.

A particular type of chicken and I enunciated that like this, like a par-

TICK-you-lar type of chicken.

The kind of chicken I like to eat is kept in a cage. It is kept in a small cage, with hundreds of other chickens. You would have no idea how many chickens were in that cage if you saw a picture of it. I wouldn't. I'm terrible at things like that. A thousand? Seventy-five? And they may have had their beaks cut off? So they don't poke each other? And that's just, that's just good business, ma'am, is what that is. Because, do you want poked chickens, ma'am? Is that something that you'd be interested in? A poked chicken? Huh. Takes all kinds I guess, and where was I, where were we? Oh, and they may be in there, and they may be fed through a slot? And I'm asking even though I know the answer? Even though this isn't a question? And it's cruel and it's inhumane, and whatever it is, it's tight and it's confining, the area is. Whatever it is, it's that, and it could be wet? You know, wet like a scene out of Hostel? I've never seen Hostel, ma'am, the movie Hostel, but I'm guessing it's like that, where everything's kind of cold and dingy and wet looking? And frightening, it's frightening, and the lights, when they're on, maybe they're flickering? Flickering wet lights? It's like the hospital in that movie Jacob's Ladder, I've seen that, ma'am, that's exactly what this is, that's where they keep these chickens. Carts with wonky wheels wheeling by, through puddles, puddles with stagnant water, with offal, and filth? And they're all crowded in there together and they're huddled and they are embarrassed, too, the chickens are, and I don't know how you do that, but you do it. I want my chickens to be embarrassed, right, and I want them to feel bad. And I also want them to feel like there might be some hope? Like there might be a way out of this, that's what I want, ma'am. And I want them to be imbued with the consciousness that there may be a way out, but not quite smart enough to even conceive of what that way out might be. Like, that's the level of intelligence I want these chickens to have and I don't know what the label on this could possibly look like, do you? What would the label on a package of chickens raised under these conditions look like? Bewildered, confined, confused, semi-conscious chickens? Is it that, is that it? I'm asking. I'm trying to specify, I'm trying to explain. This is me explaining. Look how hard this is, look how hard. And what? A label? Right, yeah, no, like I don't know what that label would look like, have no idea, haven't gotten there yet, and remember, I haven't even gotten out of bed yet. This is all, this is first thing, and also? I want these chickens to be petrified, did I mention that? I want them to be so scared, I want them with that level of consciousness, that they can kind of understand what's happening and about to happen. To them, ma'am, to them. And I want them to be absolutely fucking horrified, and I want some guy dressed like a clown maybe to jump out from behind something or something and scare the shit out of them, right before the fucking thing goes through their head, that's what I want. Right before the bolt that dully, you know, crushes their brain and skull and brain-skull, before that is released, right? Into their heads, that's the scene, that's what I want it to look like. That's what I want to have happened, and I will only eat those, because for me to eat them, for me to consume their energy, and that's really what this is, isn't it? Ma'am? It's about taking energy? From one thing to another? And that's what we're doing and if that's what it is, and I think that it is, then I want these things to be fucking petrified, because the way I see it, how can that not make me stronger? It's just logic, it's just logic, ma'am. It's an exercise in logic, that's what this is, that's what this was, here now and before in bed. It's just logic, it just makes sense and I don't make the rules, but I do play by them. And you know what I'm saying here, ma'am? Do you know the kind of chicken I'm talking about because I'll tell you, you look like you do. I knew that when you walked in, could tell when you sat down, I was like there's a lady who knows exactly the kind of chicken I'd like to eat. And that's not, and let's clear this up, that's not a sexual thing, like a come-on thing, because, right, I mean I know how that sounds. Like I'm trotting out that old line, like I'm standing here going, "No really, you just seem like a really nice person, like you know, like you'd know what kind of chickens I'd eat, like the conditions surrounding the chickens I'd eat." I know how that sounds; it isn't like that, it isn't, it isn't.

And what is this, what is that? Is that something a retarded person would say? What does it mean, do you think? And why would I say that? And this is the point, folks, and the point is this. The point is, there has to be a reason I say things like this, and it could be because I'm retarded, I don't know.

from Work

☆

Richard Makin

XXXI

We may be in need of the odd interval. Whiff of mercury rising: the instrument used consists of a flint box with sounding board; wires are stretched taut across the bridge. The postilion's head is off come dawn.

We stand on the foreshore and say no to every question. Nothing is reliable — no physical collision to the right, the south, none to the left, the north. We are about to come face to face with a stranger on the cobbled square. North signifies malefic.

I heard just one sound then the landscape must have dissolved immediately.

'With an appetite for the archaic, he is dispenser and composer of all things,' she replies.

Probably magnetism is meant. In other words, the human body suggests points of fire to which the alchemic artist endeavours to give concrete form — congealing when extracted from the kidneys, the liver, the spleen. Origin is 'made thick', from the verb. What do you want to do tomorrow, what cage harbours your usefulness?

A slight change of velocity. Eight cylinders now in narrow monobloc — coil ignition, zenith pump- fed from tank fermentation — hypnoid bevel device, front independent, rear half epileptic. . . . My own dereliction is a bye, a thrown bet in a counterfeit scene.

He was not wounded at all: the sheath of the tendon, any tissue of the body, can and will heal. Dried bark was provided to scribble upon for free.

Another lies tongue-tied beneath a blanket of pollen. The legion survives the descent in this manner, bleached bone resistant on tho paving slab. They always deceive about the market value of what they produce.

*

Lately come as evermore, sleep does not visit mine eyes et cetera — you are always in my vision, always in my skull. (Voice is scarcely the easiest option.) The first thing she says to me is you're not the right person, I never should have: you are self-saboteur, a disaster — a natural disaster, I grant you, but nonetheless. Soon she will advocate writing, cessation.

The patient is to be executed by contract. We draw lots. The apostrophe key is jammed. She is busy composing one of her lists.

I'm appointed executioner. Ascending a short flight of steps I reach the iron matrix that holds her, a starvation cage suspended above a stagnant pool. The contraption shudders and clatters, yields up the wraith before sliding into the oily waters of the tarn.

We could go back in time (perhaps) she hazards: try to make a decision, mourn the lost six of your company. The survivors arm themselves and head out for the stadium at the edge of the city. A cliff collapses into the sea, frame by frame.

These are your own rules we're following; I'm still thinking of that unpleasant scene at the bus terminus. Among your crew is one who is thus possessed, who gives himself so completely that each time you take leave of him you feel it's of no consequence whether parting is for one day, or forever.

'Gone for a wander (11.20). And then to J's café (the red one). You have the key. Go through the chalk tunnel down the green steps and straight on, wherever they deliver you. This will be our chosen place. Why did I not stray, heretofore?'

Be good, if you can't. My apparent indifference doesn't exempt me from acts of vengeance. Now I must stop.

Shutter across head in shadow, onward into terrain of ash, rust; once again we're on a journey of time and geography shackled together. The name is probably a breeder's name, preserved at a lucky moment and embedded in the heel. His head is off (the wire). Where is he then. The next station is battle-ore.

The white plain catches whatever precipitation falls to earth. In my knapsack I have my notes and favourite things.

'Is it tomorrow night, is it not tonight, I thought it was tonight.'

Walking slowly, inland to the crest — toothless, odour of urine (passed). We've just swapped the place names around.

Nothing, nothing is choreographed for tonight.

*

Estranged wife kidnaps musical the strapline read. . . . I deflate the immediate. She has never used. She chews at my cord. The day cannot hold our exchange; anything you can avoid, avoid. Are you on or off the premises? I have walked; I have been cancelled. We spent the greater part of our time in solitary.

The boy hurls an army of stones. (He and I are of the tribe of Cain.) His nature is frequently exploded, like nitroglycerine in the mouth. Our seed is mistrust; now we can do whatever we want. He's cased in leather armour, the true skin hidden beneath a toughened epidermis. I've a tendency to identify him as the son of either/or — and who is that third, walking beside you?

*

More rhetorically embellished speech at the regular Friday meet. (I've never heard of him.) Practise your inventory: a tin can with bullet, the shattered wooden box, a heap of stones, green algae floating on a creek at low tide. . . . The ruined casket is set at an angle; we are many waves from home. On the shore beside the loch is a cake of fire — relax, you don't actually lose any of your lives in the process.

Common perception: my lack of caution, random attentions whereby I carry myself off. I interrupt. You can see for miles — turn your head, and in the other direction you may peer straight through the cell wall. This is where cryogenics comes into it.

It looks as though you're set permanently against the wind (whether imminent or simply waiting). This promises to be a no-go area, yet tirelessly I list: a leguminous plant with clover-like leaves and bluish flowers, a swarm of fireflies, crimson pollen of the lily. . . . This feels like a natural break in the proceedings, nothing like it in the whole wide world.

An easy prey to habit, one boy burns in his night shroud. (What's the remedy.) His term is elastic. All gathered reckon it's a nerve, trapped.

I regard as baser yet he who is quick to please. A parcel is delivered; I break the wax seal. I roamed before I settled (the author's a Napoleon of his own making). The festival unravels — I'm jabbing at the page.

Demolish obsolete — shelf of rock, a flagellum. I foresee you going in, guns blazing, one disaster hard on another. . . . I wonder whether you'll last the outcome, the peace.

He works to undercut himself on the hard frozen ground. This seems the oldest solution on offer — to leap from the balcony, another lottery-funded suicide. The others escort him home before there's no point to the favour.

The cab driver says he knows nothing, then adds that the planets Saturn and Mars are traditionally considered to have an unfavourable influence.

*

When searched, a list is found on a scrap of paper in my pocket. During the celebrations a muscle was torn, wounded flesh surrounding an abscess — sap of acid, allied to nothing. One outlaw had a full name; it was 1882, or thereabouts. He was joined to his brother at the hip and scapula. It was 1915, or thereabouts. Others formed a notorious gang which specialized in bank and train robberies and inspired many.

One outlaw had a full name. It was 1880, or thereabouts. He was leader of a band of horse and cattle thieves and bank raiders who operated. He was eventually hanged. Such is a person of reckless courage, such is a person who shows a lack of scruples in business. She too is a person audaciously bold. Origin is late from the name.

A major mountain system is running the length of the coast. Its highest peak rises to a height of 6,960m or 22,834ft. In folklore it is always night; witches meet on the mountain and hold orgies with the devil. Origin is named after a saint.

A medium-sized, chiefly forest-dwelling old world monkey has a long face and cheek pouches for holding food. In mythology, the wife of the king and mother found a constellation near the north celestial pole, recognized by the conspicuous W pattern of its brightest stars. It is misused with a preceding letter or mineral.

See, any act of witnessing. I once was trapped under your stairs; I couldn't find the switch — a door, a corner — nothing. It's known that somewhere in England there is a grave.

More acute animosity is flaring up in our principalities. (Thank you, kindness.) It's like going home, isn't it — windows squaring up to the dark. The men are fighting over the pier. The land slips; it's apocalypse beyond the square, our collapsing boundary. The legion has mounted and refuses to withdraw — reinforcements are mustered and lock themselves into position. (Everyone appreciates a side, your underdog.) In the distance, old derelict textile, wandering dunes, a current of fine sand coursing about our ankles as we stand together at the foreshore.

It says about earshock, it says on the observant placard: 'He pummels the stove with cosmic severity' et cetera. On that very page is found the following.

*

Your generosity seems without limit; I live, as you know, by frugal means. (Visualize this book beside the shakedown in your windowless cell.) The house is the house with seven gables and is surrounded by a moat and shield of quickthorn. We reached the end of the land, finisterre, a promontory formally called. My own enclosure is flanked by a narrow alley strewn with broken glass and a false wall. If I gaze at a painting, a period of time elapses.

There is the memory of a sky with nexus of gold at the horizon, strips of rose and blue above the compass. A shallow of white mist clung to her feet as she jogged the early morning track. A satellite is reflected in each of the four windows. Their language is made of intercepting circles.

At the cloister is a herb garden quarried from a pit older than dynasty, where two granite figures face each other down. The anchor chain passes through a tube which doubles as a mortar canister, a short piece for hurling shells — see bombardier, a lifeline, matter pounding in the heart — a person who has literally ascended by falling. I was fashioned from a single lucky cast.

Of course, she says, if he hadn't been crooked, we'd never have backed him at all. And then she says, mother of God, even here one man can make a bureaucracy of his mouth.

The adamantine rock strikes fire.

Probably elvan — hard intrusive igneous found, typically porphyry. A spark. Granular dyke: an accumulation of quartz and orthoclase — fracture common or potash feldspar, monoclinic with cleavage set at right angles. . . . Debris formed on the spot, or moved by wind, as loss.

I see. The organism is condensing water from the humid air; I am myself formed on analogy of 'to swab'. Events damaged me so deep, it took a year to recover. The whole family was lodged on the roof; they were loyal.

Often I ask myself, is this a real choice or another assassination? The right hand is slightly blurred, suggesting motion. Each contestant is bound to its neighbour — an agglutination is thus composed, spongy voids on the dashboard, a hanging saint at sway, fragile reassurance.

I am not there and they will not wait for me. The planchette skates across the lead, scratching out code; I am inking every fibre. There is that sound.

He deserves more, deserves better, has not prepared himself for the undertone of mortality, recollections of someone else's boyhood. There is nothing to see murmur the summoned police persons.

*

Insomnia, action of opiates on locus coeruleus firing. Chronic activation of receptors leads to tolerance, the homeostatic mechanism compensating for changes in your manifesto.

Sheer genius: the opioid prompts the liver to manufacture morphine, which acutely inhibits firing of neurons. An occult intracellular mechanism leads to compensation and premature death, destruction by supernatural agency.

If they venture in we will have no option but to release the signal flares. No more comment, ever! (See barbarian west, the 400-1 outsider.) She is also an engineer. There is the memory of a woman on a train, making up her face. There is the memory of a woman on a jetty, turning, like the sudden inrush of a liquid.

The effect: it doesn't sound like anything I have ever experienced. I approximate. There is the mockery of a sky with a strip of gold upon which everything hinges, remembrance of a clock- tower. . . . I recall seeing the picture and thinking, my life is not this, this is full of dates all out of kilter. She tastes the inrush, the sudden arrival of something, anything.

*

A maze of pores is held together by a zip; I suppose these things happen. I thought that yesterday the garden would do, the categories would prevail. But he's in traction, the death of an obscure science, still trying to justify himself and authenticate a single moment.

The saint's fast coincides with a minimum-wage heretic festival whose rites give sanctuary to witchcraft. I need a counterpoint to this. We are estimated (it might be a bit longer, it might be a bit less). What he can't keep up with, he leaves behind.

'Bring them down, the stars down to earth.'

For example, Delta Cassiopeia. He wears bilateral tassels that dangle from his scalp; at base, he can seem like an actual person. Hang on, just in case we're parted, always.

You're losing all connection to the local, the time that place forgot quips my journeyman. Maximum curvature of spine is permitted, the crew hunched over their precious instruments, connecting them to someone else's mutability.

I'm glad you're breathing here with me, unwired among the strangers, all the random prototypes. I never wanted to stop: hard seal of wax in the canal, the rudimentary valve — very lively coda at the entrance to the interior, and I with no ear to speak of.

*

Face in the pillow. [*Deadpan.*]

'Have you still got that metal neck brace.'

'Who are, who are all those people.'

An object has been made by pouring molten metal into a mould, but I can't keep up with the action; for example, I don't remember that totemic nerve. And then she murmurs no such community as things, something like that. Much later, she will erase the guilty sentence.

Nerves impartial today, gentle as hawk or gyrfalcon — one-third of a pipe, a cask or abandoned vessel of capacity. Is there room? Sort yourself out.

a) A wood pigeon (sound).

b) A sequence of three cards of the same suit.

c) A third of something, anything.

d) A fencing piston.

e) A pontoon ferry (grudge).

f) The office of that hour, the terce said or chanted, distress of stillness.

g) The third hour of the day, ending at nine.

h) Of a field, divided, each of a separate tincture.

i) A system of betting by which the opponent must be identified in a pre-established order.

j) A race to which this system binds.

k) A subordinate rib springing from the intersection of two other ribs.

I am one-third smaller than the female and hatch at close of day. A tube leads from the middle ear to the cleft, venal at the heart.

This seems the most historic solution on offer. The contestant falls into a series of pale, regrettable weeks. Nearby is a boundary wall, thatched with peat and reeds from the marsh — our common crossing, turf wars over territory, a particular sphere of influence — a borderer: selectman, marchmen.

A recurring event — the boundary stone, that which does not concern others. Retreat is signalled through our contents: schedule, ritual, temporal rift. Quarks are forecast, not directly observed.

And basically this idea consists of three words: pig. A sense of place arrived with him — a ceremony, riding about the rim of our principality. (There's clearly a page missing here.) This is what they used to do. There are caves; there is a torch — there is ochre, red and blue. I hope we are safe to here — it's *de profundis* time — a gull crashes into the window and the temperature suddenly drops; that's the cue to walk on my hands. A cry is followed by another cry.

This passage contains some words that don't belong. For example, we met with unexpected resistance: the island acts like a centrifuge. I detect the rustle of tongue, leafy elocutions — a slow dig, domestic archaeologies, the way of redundant x-ray — one long howl, a terracotta bowl of mercury set upon the floor at the foot of the bed. We are taking a detour (a not unpleasant deviation). I must admit, I am not actual.

The bodies detected have possible astronomical significance, but there's no apparent conflict — monuments with a view, billions of doubters below.

Spraying himself with repellent, he straps on the harvesting knife — a broad three-foot blade with a sharp crescent hook at the end. (You are not patient enough.) He's sure the correct treatment could not be a life of relentless distraction.

Nowadays, folk have to check their own keys, their own trolley (don't get me wrong, Wednesday's not usually a bad day). More and more he resembles, leaves a flood of semen on the faux-leather upholstery.

I've nothing to add to this; some sensations can't be articulated. There are plans to mix modernity with sheer panic, or at least put a stop to this ceaseless footfall. Your match is a spent match.

Nonetheless, there is magnetic intensity and direction in your prehistoric objection, ankle deep in mud and slush — not here, not now. My neurons have today returned to their normal firing rates.

Are you going to sing or talk, or is this a transcript? You missed a couple of words. The lady spectre was here, I swear, now absent of a sudden.

When he finally deigns to speak, I have the feeling he knows just about everything. Quick, I'm enjoying the neutral at present, this dank chalky stratum. The entity acts up now and again, then a sudden unforeseen gesture and it stops.

I ignore. He is not A and he is not B — we are safe to here, I think. A series of coils is burnt into wood, according to a centrifugal pattern.

'It is the dish which makes the hat.'

Ectopia. Morbid naming of parts, the wandering womb — a depression in the face filled with putrescent matter, neural assault. . . . Calm yourself, calm yourself upon a grassy ridge of land, the gently sloping outburst — wrap legs around her legs, sliding toward the lower plummet (No.15). There is an absence of anecdote, an absence of parable; I was initially intended for the apology at the end. A great inrush of fluid occurred, yes.

I try to break into a cabin in the dark, and in the process lose the compass embedded in my lung — finding now a place to pass the night will be complicated. On the final stretch a few furlongs out, a strange buzzing from the corpse nearby on elevated ground. You've been up there every day since it happened; it's a question of teasing out the details. I've been attached ever since the desert.

The nearest person to the stun grenade has to volunteer. I am to perform the final act. There then follows a series of deft feints and touches, whereupon she emerges from the game with her identity bent backwards.

I'm the only true gambler in the room. It hath a long bony tail, this primitive avian reptile.

In spite of all this, the patient's fine — seismic aftershock burrowing into the skull.

Antinomy, the gloomy archaeology of a tryst. We agree to meet; an appointment is made at an appointed spot. I wait in person at a prearranged bend in time; I'm blessed with the hunter's tempo and instinct.

Say nothing, perfect radio. I notice that no one has noticed my silence, the most supple compliment one could hope for. By this I mean folk did see and hear and they did not see and hear.

The incident.

It is here and it is affective, but not as a remembered event: oblivious apprehension rather than comprehension (i.e. the will to interpret, to convert all things to interference). I got to wear a badge and a cap, to whose authority the whole province is subject; this is contrary to our usual custom. The archivist is required to busy himself with a whole variety of matters, simply to provide for his own needs, submerging forever all that is not.

She is credited with inventing the nocturne. (Your hands are cold.) She abandoned the maestro and shortly thereafter fell blind in torment. Nonetheless, she outlived him by a wilderness or two.

You hang your head. She levitates into the air while violently shaking the infant; both of us are cities of the mind. (I say this, just in case we're ever parted.) Her friendship is hydraulic — it has not yet won my compass.

If I place myself in front of her, my arteries begin to knot; we have been attached ever since the desert — the backwash of meaning never stops. I was the last person.

*

You're being really brave. (Whisper two, sedative of Yes.) Taste of another's breath, another on the tongue, piercing the mouthpiece. She had the pale blue eyes of a wolf. I should do something about this but can no longer tell what is needed; all the life long, my orders have been cracked.

We must hold on to the unsustainable for twelve more weeks — after that, it's promised that we fade. I use as an excuse the first object that presents itself to my vision, in this case a tiny organism composed of two genetically distinct tissues (protein and alien). My own parts are fabricated, built of disparity. Still they shape their house of fire.

I can't tell you what I whispered to them, murmuring my own treatise: bad company, language and the like, crumbs of broken bread. The Greeks call it a spectral hand, i.e. the one who stoops to speak. Theoretical predictions based on our existence have been rejected experimentally.

Outside once more, beside a watercourse — any channel for fluid will do — a line of seed, the sluice.

Note to self, restore angelic upcry.

Work is published by Equus Press in 2020

2 Poems

☆

Mari-Lou Rowley

Why Walk If You Can Fly

With a leap so light just lift yourself
  up
like a leaf, like a dancer.

Gentle thermal inhale and exhale
of the body's rise and lowering
into a cradle in the rock, wind break,
resting place, belvedere,
  sentinel control.

Oh the view from up here!
The scampering baroque adagio and arpeggio
of voices, towers, cities
  rising, falling.

Look! Over there—
small humans hide in a bush,

over there—
a river quivers with the wrong kind of fish.

Turn your head to the right. Particulate haze
of a lazy afternoon, burgers and beer,
 wildfires.

Utility Program ∎ Alpha

This restlessness is a need to write down this restlessness ∎
Walruses stampede to the edge of receding ice flows ∎ Synapses
tinged with embedded jingoisms, too much blubber ∎ What parts of
the mechanism are you prepared to forfeit?

Amygdala dalliance in basal ganglia bandwidth, in the bling of an
eyelash, detached from seeing ∎ Multiheaded daemons monitoring
changes in host states ∎ Blink once to acknowledge federate
clusters ∎

Back on the ice flow walruses fin the water, monitor changes in
hostile states when the dictator bares his chest ∎ In the grand
schema Web profiles are small utility programs ∎ To escape
the cluster nodes, go out. Look up!

2 Poems

☆

Jennifer K. Dick

Crank

What are we unable to locate, if shifted a few centimeters? The encounter with the lover happens after years frequenting the same venues. To dance and take in light. To burn. The house, abandoned, tells its own stories to itself. Nostalgia for the months of diners. In the dream the cactus stretches prickly tendrils round her ankle. There is no turning back from the destruction of the mines. The Romans pack up what they can before the advancing army's arrival. The stockroom, laden with goods, begins its slumber. There is a mindfulness in the meridian, matinal, mockingbird, morningtide. Crisp and across-stream past le chardon said over and over, she hears cauldron, brewed remains of eye of newt, stirred entrails, a reading in the seer's pastel blue eye. Adrift, aloft, the wavelift of her seeks to speak against the roar of propellers, recollections of cicada, leapfrog, grasshoppers snatched by grey cats. She once woke at a snail's pace to see the displaced nest had roused an angry swarm.

MOD (Maximum Operating Depth)

1

incandescent nightwave
luminous default
to take (me) (her)
undersurface: wetsuit
leaking icicles
serendipity of this enclosure
bubble-blooming
fissure-resisting
release

2

incumbent un-
encumbered into belonging's
foreshadowing: letterscapes
what is feared / seared
into marble
echo insonorized to
mute out, meander into
indigo needle-rooting
growths as inhaled
dandelion-prickling forms
of mold gasp
encroach

3

seraphim centurions
crux criss-crossing
reversalism as in
humanism's faux-universalism
weft along the concretizing
ledge of her carapace

4

conversion rolled into
cloudscape's frontispiece:
ledger lunar reminiscence
of a typecast fiber-optic
illusion of architecture
stairs or a strain of
astringent accolations
soured confessions of
awaiting rooms this way
is no out

5

concomitant corollaries
negation in the gathered-among
above deck overreach
sonorous discontinuities
unwarranted enticement
"what is?" she asks, parts
a small rectangular card
blue then winter's pink
stethoscope chest-held
grip or to grope in
the medicinal box for
—she says—wards or
words or a berserk motor
turns over, runs
undercarriage

6

wavelit / length
a measuring of liquefied
powders: her night-light
photo-exposure
developing as a
near-extinction event

a species (I) enter
a game of naming
normative figures formed
from sepulchral umbra
eye-scanner hook netted
in the betweensea
below ballast ocean
rafts to riverruns
the mouth insists
on this opening

7

curlicue curtailed catacomb
methodology of micro-
management
accessed madness
mockingbird aboard
the weight of flight
waves bobbers nets
a hat adrift billowing
downsail prow or aft
in the lightening bolt
stingray-path along
sea-mottled sandbars
staircases in ship-hulls
along locks, harbors
masking foghorn alarms
this radiant
penumbra

3 Poems

☆

Ann Tweedy

Breast Cancer's Origin Storie(s)

1. The time in Scotland in the dorm when you made chocolate mousse in an aluminum pan during Christmas vacation because there were no bowls and scrapings of pan curled into the mousse and you threw it out but tasted it first.

2. The prescription acne medicine you took for years that the FDA had only approved for blood pressure, one of the side effects of which was painful and swollen breasts.

3. Living for three years in the East Bay with its elevated breast cancer risk (that you didn't know of at the time) in order to attend law school.

4. The stress of being laid off from university teaching when law schools began to fail and how the threat of lay-off stretched for over a year and coalesced with a desperate hope that enough students would enroll to turn things around.

5. How you fell in love just after being laid off but didn't know what to do because you were already long married and the new love didn't want to be involved with anyone in that situation.

6. The years during which you used antiperspirant, which contains aluminum.

7. How you had your first and only child late--at age 38.

8. How your BMI was within normal range, though barely.

9. How you were tormented by feelings of failure and thoughts of suicide while being laid off and while falling in love.

10. How you lived with that torment and did nothing to minimize it.

11. The busy years of teaching during which you went to the gym only once a week and ran or biked once a week. The not enough.

12. The not feeling loved as a child.

13. The sense of having to take care of everything always because no one else would.

14. The not being able to flee a relationship when it turned ugly.

15. The belief that you could win back love and thereby prove lovableness.

16. The years you ate lunches at work out of plastic microwavable dishes.

17. The time your husband heated hot fudge in a plastic bowl that wasn't supposed to be microwaved and you ate it anyway, as a show of love.

18. The mold in the house where you grew up.

19. The termite treatment done in the apartment when you were

pregnant.

20. The grandfather who hated women and therefore hated teenage-you, the stepmother who counted your father's every minute and every penny, the mother who thought the police were plotting to rape you, the quietness of going to high school thinking no one would ever talk to you, the loneliness that seeped into your cells then.

21. The mutation in your genes that has yet to be identified.

Travelers

I think of the salmon spawning who so long to lay eggs in their natal streams that they will literally kill themselves crashing against obstructions to get there. "[R]eturning adults must apply their olfactory memory to discriminate among increasingly similar water sources." What would it be to have a home so indisputably yours that you would die to get there? Of course it's no joke—many many salmon die instead of arriving and each year the runs get smaller and smaller. On the White River, for instance, chinook may become trapped in the voids of the dam apron or "injure or kill themselves . . . jumping against . . . [its] exposed rebar and broken timbers." Others are killed or injured "trying to locate the fish ladder." Ten to twenty percent of chinook hauled upstream of the dam have head lesions, and forty percent of those hauled "are not accounted for in spawning surveys," suggesting pre-spawning mortality. For years, I have deliberately moved from state to state without arriving anywhere. And yet carried a hope of arriving. The house I spent from nine months to eighteen in has been bulldozed but the smell I remember is mustiness. Sometimes I open a bin or box filled with things from that house and immediately know that smell—choking and comforting at the same time. I have often thought of the salmon's need—an ineluctable desire to live and to die. At the same time--or in short succession. And my own restlessness—a ship that sails me.

The Aspen

The aspen's root mass
might stretch 100 acres, sending up shoots hither
and yon. No one knows how long each root mass
may last—live stems say little about other identical
twins—but Pando in Southern Utah
has survived 80,000 years and some aspen devotees guess
forever is a possibility. Forever to suck up water
and nutrients and send them back
in dropped leaves. Forever to wave one's arms
in the breeze, to quiver leaves
on their petioles
the way dog fur expels water.

The ski lodge promises: *Roll your unused
days over with our worry-free guarantee.*

The aspen can grow and regrow multiple bodies.
It sends up shoots from its root promise.
When a fire fells a forest, the aspen
breathes underground even if all its soldiers
are downed. When *fomes igniarius*
rots heartwood, flammulated owl
and yellow-bellied sapsucker move in.
The grey matter down below sends
another emissary to sunshine and cankers and birth.

The last time I saw you, I was lighter,
in better shape, lacked reading glasses,
had a higher ratio of brown to grey,
believed in the possibility of happiness.
Nothing girds me from underneath
but ordinary gravity—she who pulls
everyone toward a final embrace.
Would that you and I could roll our separate
days between then and now into a finite together.

The integral actuality of human experience

☆

Ian Brinton

Walking, a love story, Toby Olson (Occidental Square Books, 2020)
Death Sentences, Toby Olson (Shearsman Books, 2019)

Telescope, selected poems, Michael Heller (New York Review Books, 2019)

Toby Olson's novel is of course about movement. The movement involved in the physical process of walking reflects the movement forward from a burial in the past to an awakened awareness of the present. The overriding importance of this movement is emphasised in the epigraph to *Walking*, a quotation from Xenophon:

> Excess of grief for the dead is madness; for it is an injury to the living, and the dead know it not.

That reflection is presented with uncompromising clarity in one of the early poems in Olson's collection *Death Sentences* many of which are addressed to his wife, Miriam, who died in 2014:

> About life and death, about dreaming,
> about the picture of you with your new bicycle,
> about memory:
> the dead's messages
> written into the skins of the living.
> ('Standard-18, *There Will Never Be Another You'*)

The act of walking might seem sometimes to be the pacing of a prison cell or the claustrophobic circularity of Van Gogh's 1890 painting of 'Prisoners Exercising'. As Olson's narrator Aphrodite sets out to escape the eyes of her father she is in almost constant motion even walking up and down the aisles of the occasional bus she travels on 'getting nowhere, while the bus took me somewhere'. Trapped between the room of her dying mother and the eerily penetrating gaze of her father, Aphrodite 'would walk out of the oppression of that space into the relative freedom of another'. The close confinement of her father's gaze imprisons her wherever she may try to escape to and 'he would follow me, sit me down again, then penetrate me with those eyes of his, and I would once again have to rise and walk away into other rooms and free spaces. Again and again.' However, as with the prisoners in the exercise yard she remains confined in spite of the movement:

> Time for a little counting. Each step, up to five-hundred, then back again to zero. Something to do. Like humming. I am not bored, nor anxious, nor do I have hopes of getting somewhere. I am just moving.

On the first page of this remarkably terrifying and uplifting novel we are told that the narrator 'walked here from Wisconsin' and I found myself unable not to recall the opening of William Faulkner's *Light in August* which began with Lena's optimistic search for the father of her soon-to-be-born child:

> Sitting beside the road, watching the wagon mount the hill toward her, Lena thinks, 'I have come from Alabama: a fur piece. All the way from Alabama a-walking. A fur piece.

However, the movement in Olson's novel might also be

worth a comparison with the early statement from Paul Auster's dystopian vision *In the Country of Last Things* where the narrator warned us that when we walk through the streets we must take care to remember to take only one step at a time, to avoid falling:

> Your eyes must be constantly open, looking up, looking down, looking ahead, looking behind, on the watch for other bodies, on your guard against the unforeseeable.

In Toby Olson's novel Aphrodite as narrator seems initially to be in charge of the story which she tells but, as she is increasingly compelled to recognise, 'these people that I have created are beginning to move on, to move away from my control'. Her awareness foreshadows the novelist's own words in the closing pages of the book as he tells the reader:

> She speaks directly to us, and as she moves along, she creates characters before our eyes. But then something happens, and these characters step away from her, move beyond her control, take on a life of their own.

In those closing pages Olson also pays tribute to Gilbert Sorrentino's 1979 novel *Mulligan Stew* and it might be worth recalling that in an interview with Donald Phelps published in *Vort 6* some five years before that novel's appearance Sorrentino had compared writing prose to 'shovelling coal':

> You have a plan, of course, and each day the plan becomes more complicated. You have to concentrate on what you're up to and then you have to remember that there are things that you have written earlier that you want to revise...

These revisions permit a novel to generate its own movement forward and there is an increasing awareness of what might have been different in that past which has led to this present. It is as though we tread upon the bones of the long dead and 'those who are gone / are still truculent after passage / into cocoons in memory's storage' ('Death Sentences, 6').

This close connection between the past and the present

is central to Michael Heller's comment upon his own 'urge to write'
as he described it in his memoir *Living Root* (SUNY Press, 2000)
as the 'setting down of a word in the blankness of space, as the
dropping of an anchor in the abyss'. A few years earlier in his 1994
essay 'Encountering Oppen', Michael Heller had brought his eye
to focus on what it is that makes us who we are. He suggested
that every individual and occasion in one's life becomes 'an actual
influence, a scene of instruction, a mentoring of sorts'. Thirty years
before, in 1965 his movements to avoid the 'deceptive enchantments
of language' had led him to resign his position as the head technical
writer for a major corporation in order to board a Yugoslavian
freighter that would take him from New York to Europe. In his
journey across the ocean, having set keel to breakers, Heller settled
in a small house in a small village in Spain and whilst unpacking
his books he took up his copy of George Oppen's *The Materials*
(New Directions, 1962). The last poem of that collection, 'Leviathan',
opened with the line 'Truth also is the pursuit of it':

> I read the line over and over, like a chant, feeling a raw ache
> in my chest. What did the words mean to me? I had only the
> vaguest idea, but also a sense of wanting to weep. I calmed
> myself down and began to decipher my response. I took
> the "it" of the line as art, hunger, the clarification of the very
> confusion I was experiencing.

That hunger for clarification is the thread which runs seamlessly
through this new selection of Heller's work and it gives tangible
reality to the words of Walter Benjamin which Heller had placed
as the epigraph to his 1997 essay 'Notes on Lyric Poetry or at the
Muse's Tomb':

> Translating the language of things into that of humans
> entails not only translating silence into audibility; it means
> translating the nameless into the name.

Telescope presents us with a wide selection of poems
ranging from the mid-1960s to the recently written 'Colloquia' with
its opening reference to that haunting presence of Oppen which has
pursued the poet down the years:

"World, World," you wrote,
as though martyred to the visible,

the words one chose
would have to say it.

If the famous rosy-fingered dawn
existed, it existed to be proclaimed,

as did the catalog of phrases to embrace,

sheer gorgeousness and vibratory
power of words

to upend those imprisoning
geometries of the conventional.

That "World, World" offers a murmuring echo of that use of 'it' which
had so moved Michael Heller back in the mid-1960s and it provides
a frame within which the developing poetry of a man committed to
dropping an anchor into the abyss can be realised with the type of
clarity a reader would wish for from a serious selection of a poet's
work.

In Toby Olson's fourteen poem sequence 'Etudes' the literal
is transcribed as he and Miriam found themselves in a new city:

pining for those earlier days
in which what's left behind is prelude
that remains still in memory

That stillness, captured so often by George Oppen and Charles
Reznikoff, is juxtaposed in Olson's work with the days which 'are
counted toward an ending'. In Michael Heller's awareness of
movement which he contemplates in 'Thinking of Mary' (1997) he
celebrates the world of journeying as Mary Oppen moves into a new
life after her husband's death:

You moved from
the bedroom shared with him into a smaller space, futon

on the floor, as though recalibrating yourself. Perhaps
you were listening there for the new life growing, growing

back like a circle on itself or like the ocean's recurrent tidal
    sweeps.

Poems by Stéphane Mallarmé
translated by Ian Brinton
and Michael Grant (Muscaliet)

☆

Ellen Dillon

In the scholarly notes accompanying his 1870 prose translation
of Edger Allen Poe's 'The Raven,' Stéphane Mallarmé assesses
his own attempt as follows: "here is a copy chancing no aim other
than rendering a few of the extraordinary sound-effects of the
original music, and here and there maybe the feeling itself." The
modest surface of the claim is troubled by the sheer ambition of
recapturing the poem's sound and feeling in another language.
Ian Brinton, discussing the working method employed by Michael
Grant and himself in their translations from French in 'Golden
Handcuffs Review' #23, describes their aims in seemingly more
expansive terms: "we felt that our translations must attempt to make
a construction of energy with which to convey the active experience
of a foreign original text." This nest of processes and abstractions,
worthy of Mallarmé himself, would seem to promise a recursive and
somewhat detached reading experience. However, it is the material,
almost tangible, qualities of this book that linger with the reader.

The first of these is the French blue cover, overlaid with a
manuscript page from 'Un Coup de Dés,' with the book's lower-case
title dwarfed by the block capital rendering of 'LE HASARD,' priming

the reader to the role of chance in the layout and language of the work between these covers. In the book's first work of chance, the dazzling azure of the cover is leached from the text through the omission of versions of Mallarmé's bluest numbers, 'Tristesse d'Eté' and 'Les Fenêtres.' It is singularly fitting to the source poems that their signature colour sings itself through absence in these pages. In a further daring move, the greeting of 'Salut' that opens *Les Poésies* emerges as a 'Pledge' two thirds of the way through Brinton and Grant's *poems*. These gestures, together with the decision to occhew facing-page source poems, ensure that this construction stands as a book in its own right, offering its reader an experience inflected, but not entirely subsumed, by its origins.

It is, unfortunately, near impossible for a reader with long familiarity with the words of the source poems to approach this work with any pure sense. Instead, they will spend much time picking fights with individual word choices for reasons that are at least as autobiographical as they are lexical. For a reader who was awakened, literally, from mid-lecture lethargy by the sonic magic of the 'Sonnet en -yx,' that poem's 'aboli bibelot' seems diminished in its new form as an 'abolished plaything.' However, this same version offers some deft echoes to deflect from the impossibility of recreating the source poem's dense sound patterning in English. To this end, 'brûlé par le Phénix' is rendered 'cindered by the Phoenix' to reflect the following line's 'cinerary urn.'

These poems are propelled by the tensions generated by the need to make constant choices, at the level of the word or line, upon which all other possibilities will hinge. In this sense every poem is inflected by a version of the crisis of the suspended dice roll of 'Un Coup De Dés,' crystalized in the decision to hedge the title as 'A Roll of the Dice [OR] The Die is Cast.' While the second title, evoking Caesar's 'alea jacta est,' suggests that the Rubicon has been crossed, the juxtaposition of titles reminds the reader that, in translation, crossing is a process and one that, Zeno-like, resists completion.

The closing lines of this poem capture the book's play of the beautiful and the baffling. Choosing 'shining and considering' for 'brillant et méditant' offers a sonic and etymological riff on the previous stanza's 'sidereal,' while turning 'avant de s'arrêter' into 'before settling' lengthens the stanza's string of gerunds into a chain of potential movement that is not within the power of the more static, adjectival French present participle. After this movement comes the still moment of the final line, 'Toute Pensée émet un Coup de Dés,' here rendered 'All thought admits Just the Roll of the Dice.' It is, no doubt, reader-specific whimsy to hear ready-made pastry in the proximity of 'Just' and 'Roll.' 'Just' does, however, seem an odd insertion and one that, taken with the choice of 'admit' rather than 'emit' for the verb, fundamentally alters the sense and orientation of the line. Where 'émet' unleashes movement outward, with the dice roll and its exponential chain of chance radiating from the thought, 'admit' suggests both restricted movement inwards and sanctioning, with the insertion of 'Just' reinforcing a sense of limiting or foreclosing possibilities that sits uneasily both with the source line and with the openness of the poem's English titles.

This kind of quibbling is one of the great joys of reading new translations of beloved poems, providing momentum for the kind of 'active experience' Brinton and Grant wish to construct in their translations. It is testament to their achievement that the poems are robust and flexible enough to withstand, even thrive, under such pressure, making a place for themselves in an infinite chain of acts of translating emanating from Mallarmé's *Poésies*.

Macrocosm, Microcosm and Memorable Language

I Want To Write an Honest Sentence
by Susan M. Schultz. Talisman House.
64 Pages. $15.95. ISBN: 978-1-58498-136-7

☆

Jesse Glass

Before writing this review I was unfamiliar with Susan M. Schultz's poetry. I knew her as the editor of Tinfish and Tinfish Press but I had never really read her poetry. What I didn't suspect was that for years she had been building an ambitious literary structure that was based on journal-keeping and that the book I was about to examine was a section of that epic-in-progress. No wonder, then, that I had to play catch-up in order to see what she was doing; to understand that the word cards of Schultz had been used to equally good effect in earlier projects like her *Trahearne Meditations*, and in her powerful *Dementia Blog* in which she grapples with the effects of disease on a member of her family.

What first drew me to the word cards in *I Want To Write an Honest Sentence* was the language. Susan M. Schultz mentioned in one of her generous e-mail exchanges with me that she had been a Wallace Stevens reader earlier in her career and it shows. Here, for example, is a passage from a card/meditation dated 31 October 2017:

...Not every sentence matters but they're all material, like the scarlet yarn that emerges from a chicken's entrails, turning butchery into narrative as per always. To tell a story is to lose it like a lock or to hide beneath it. To pick the story is to indict its tellers, draw them out of their Virginia mansions...

And another from the same card:

...The flag of our disposition is a deposition. Fake news is true insofar as someone calls it false, and false is true when it leads us down long corridors past room service and into the gunman's suite, now set off with police tape...

And yet another:

...What are these tender buttons but triggers we curl our fingers around, like a baby's hand our own. Tender is not the word, unless we consider the offer a good one...

Those examples are only from one word card and the book is 64 pages long!

At one point in our e-communication, I'd mentioned how entering one of her poems was like stepping into Tolstoi's *War and Peace*. There is the same feeling of the private taking place against a backdrop of historical events and those events in turn affecting the private again. This process works itself out remarkably well in *I Want To Write an Honest Sentence*.

I do have a problem with the lack of notes, and wish they'd been included in the book. On the other hand, Susan M. Schultz answers almost every question one might have about the situations both public and personal of which she writes in such an amazing way directly on her blog, and often just as directly on other Internet platforms. With daily increases in the power of A.I. and the invasion of the Internet by businesses and governments and the Net's steady evolution from a wonderful liberating tool to a buyer and seller of the information we leave behind us, and the consequent on-going diminishment of personal privacy, I wish that all of us would sometimes be less expansive. Like the coronavirus with which the world is currently struggling as it attempts to adapt to and eradicate the menace, yet another 'Science Fiction seeming' problem hovers on the horizon in this new century, I fear.

Notes on Contributors

Andrea Augé is an art director (print & film), photographer, artist, designer and activist for peace and justice.

Ian Brinton co-edits *Tears in the Fence* and *SNOW* and is involved with the Modern Poetry Archive at the University of Cambridge. His recent publications include a *festschrift for J.H. Prynne* (Shearsman Books) and a translation of selected poems of Mallarmé (Muscaliet Press). He is now at work on translating a selection of the poetry of Paul Valéry.

Jennifer K. Dick is an author, translator, readings curator for *Ivy Writers Paris*, residency co-organizer for *Ecrire L'Art* with La Kunsthalle Mulhouse, and assistant professor of American Literature at the Université de Haute Alsace, Mulhouse, France. Her books include *Lilith: A Novel in Fragments* (Corrupt Press, 2019), *Circuits* (Corrupt, 2013) and *Florescence* (University of GA Press, 2004). A mixed French-English and Italian language book, *That Which I Touch Has No Name* is forthcoming from Eyewear Press, London in October 2020. She has also published 6 chap/artbooks and since 2015 she has become increasingly involved in collaboration with dancers and visual artists. In 2020, poems from her next manuscript, *SHELF*

BREAK, appeared on Jerome Rothenberg's "Poems and Poetics" series, and in *Jacket2, Volt, Tears in The Fence*, and now here in *Golden Handcuffs*.

Ellen Dillon is a writer and teacher from Ireland. Her pamphlet *Excavate (Poems after Pasolini)* has just been published by Oystercatcher Press and her book *Sonnets to Malkmus* is available from Sad Press. Her poems have appeared in a range of journals in the UK and Ireland from *Adjacent Pineapple* to *Zarf*. She has completed a PhD on abstraction in contemporary poetry, focusing on the work of Peter Gizzi and Peter Manson, at the School of English in Dublin City University, and now works as a secondary school French and English teacher in Limerick.

Jesse Glass is the author of seven books of poetry, prose-poetry visual poetry and plays. His most recent publication is a limited edition object/poem titled *After Heraclitus*, which consists of a book of translations from Heraclitus as well as meditations on graffiti in two simultaneous registers of voice, and a real fossil fish with one of the Greek philosopher's fragments etched upon it. The book is dedicated to Banksy and is published by ZimZalla. Glass continues to work on *Nothing Epic: The Complete Gaha Noas Zorge* among other projects.

Michael Grant has edited both *T.S. Eliot: The Critical Heritage* and *The Raymond Tallis Reader*. He has also co-translated two chapbooks of the poems of Yves Bonnefoy and a selection of the poems of Stéphane Mallarmé with Ian Brinton.

Hank Lazer's most recent books of poetry are *Poems That Look Just Like Poems* and *Slowly Becoming Awake*. He is finishing *What Were You Thinking? - Essays 2009-2020*.

Richard Makin is a writer and artist. He studied painting at the Royal Academy, London. His publications include the fictions *Concussion Protocols* (Alienist), *Mourning* (Equus Press), *Dwelling* (Reality Street), *Forword* (Equipage) and *Universlipre* (Equipage). His next novel is *Work*, to be published by Equus during 2020; excerpts from this book are serialized online by the publisher, and have appeared in *Golden Handcuffs Review* and *Tears In The Fence*. He is a regular contributor to *Alienist* magazine. A further work of fiction, *Martian*, is published by *if p then q* in 2021. Richard lives in St Leonards on the south coast of England.

Brian Marley's novel, *Apropos Jimmy Inkling*, was published in 2019 by Grand Iota. *The Shenanigans*, a book of short fiction, will follow later this year.

John Muckle lives in London and works as a teacher. In the eighties he initiated the Paladin poetry imprint, and was general editor of its flagship anthology, *The New British Poetry*. He has published fiction, poetry and criticism, including *Cyclomotors, London Brakes, My Pale Tulip, Little White Bull: British Fiction in the 50s and 60s*, and his most recent poetry collection, *Mirrorball*. His new stories are from a forthcoming book, *Late Driver* (Shearsman, 2020).

John Olson has published numerous books of poetry and prose poetry, including *Dada Budapest, Larynx Galanxy,* and *Backscatter: New and Selected Poems*. He has also published four novels: *In Advance of the Broken Justy, The Seeing Machine, The Nothing That Is,* and *Souls of Wind*. His essays have appeared in numerous publications, including *The American Scholar, KYSO Flash* and *Writing On Air. Weave of the Dream King,* a collection of prose poems, is forthcoming from Black Widow Press.

Roberta Olson has had poetry included in numerous journals and the anthology "As If it Fell From the Sun" Etherdome Press. She lives in Seattle with writer John Olson and Athena.

A central figure in the international avant-garde for fifty years, **Rochelle Owens** is a poet, playwright, translator, and video artist. She has published seventeen books of poetry, including *Hermaphropoetics, Drifting Geometries* (Singing Horse Press), *Out of Ur: New and Selected Poems* (Shearsman), *Solitary Workwoman* and *Luca, Discourse on Life and Death* (both published by Junction Press). She is the author of four collections of plays and also edited *Spontaneous Combustion: Eight New American Plays*. She translated Liliane Atlan's *The Passersby*. Owens has been a recipient of five Village Voice Obie awards and Honors from the New York Drama Critics Circle. A pioneer in the American experimental theatre, her plays have been presented at Le Festival d'Avignon and the Berlin Theatre Festival. She is widely known as one of the most innovative and controversial writers of this century, whose groundbreaking work has influenced subsequent experimental poets and playwrights.

Lily Robert-Foley is Associate Professor of Translation Studies at the University of Paul-Valéry Montpellier 3. She is the author of *Jiji*, a novel in prose poems and conceptual writing (Omnia Vanitas Press, 2016), *Money, Math and Measure* (*Essay Press* chapbook series, 2016), *m*, a book of poetry-critique-collage (Corrupt Press, 2013), and *graphemachine*, a chapbook of visual poetry (Xcrolage, 2013). She also translates poetry and has released two book-length translations by Claude Ber and Sophie Loizeau from To Press. She is a member of Outranspo, an international group of experimental translators. If interested in reading the complete version of her novel extracted in this issue of GHR, please contact lilyrobertfoley@gmail.com

Mari-Lou Rowley has encountered a timber wolf, come between a black bear and her cub, interviewed an Italian astronaut, found over 50 four-leaf clovers, and published nine collections of poetry. Her most recent book, *Unus Mundus* (Anvil Press) was nominated for three Saskatchewan Book Awards and was Second Prize Winner in the John V. Hicks Long Manuscript Competition. Her work has appeared internationally in literary, arts, and science-related journals including the *Journal of Humanistic Mathematics* and *Aesthetica Magazine's* Creative Works Competition anthology (UK). A forthcoming book of poetry *Numen*ℝ*ology*, will be published by Anvil Press in Spring 2021. Rowley is in the final throes of completing a PhD dissertation in social media, neuro-phenomenology and empathy at the University of Saskatchewan, Canada.

Susan M.Schultz is author of *Dementia Blog* and *"She's Welcome to Her Disease": Dementia Blog, vol. 2*, as well as several volumes of *Memory Cards*. Her most recent book is *I Want to Write an Honest Sentence*, from Talisman (2019). She founded Tinfish Press, which she edited from 1995-2019. She lives in Hawai`i, and cheers for the St. Louis Cardinals.

Ben Slotky is a frequent contributor to *Golden Handcuffs Review* whose work has appeared in the *Santa Monica Review, Barrelhouse, Hobart, Numero Cinq*, and many other publications. His first collection, *Red Hot Dogs, White Gravy*, was published by Chiasmus in 2010 and republished by Widow & Orphan in 2017. Included here are selections from his novel *An Evening of Romantic Lovemaking*, which will be published by Dalkey Archive press in January 2021.

Philip Terry was born in Belfast, and is a poet, translator, and a writer of fiction. He has translated the work of Georges Perec and Raymond Queneau, and is the author of the novel *tapestry*, shortlisted for the Goldsmiths Prize. His poetry volumes include *Oulipoems, Shakespeare's Sonnets, Dante's Inferno,* and *Dictator*, a version of the *Epic of Gilgamesh* in Globish. He is currently translating Ice Age signs from the caves at Lascaux. *The Penguin Book of Oulipo*, which he edited, appeared in 2019.

Ann Tweedy's first full-length book, *The Body's Alphabet*, was published by Headmistress Press in 2016. It earned a Bisexual Book Award in Poetry and was also a finalist for a Lambda Literary Award and for a Golden Crown Literary Society Award. Ann also has published two chapbooks, the first of which is being reissued by Seven Kitchens Press later this year. Additionally, her hybrid chapbook, *A Registry of Survival*, is forthcoming from Last Word Press. Her poems have appeared in *Rattle, Literary Mama, Clackamas Literary Review*, and elsewhere, and she has been nominated for two Pushcart Prizes and a Best of the Net Award. An attorney by day, Ann has devoted her career to serving Native Tribes, and she recently moved from Washington State to South Dakota to join the faculty at University of South Dakota School of Law.

Curtis White is a novelist and social critic. His most recent books are *Lacking Character*, a novel, and *Living in a World That Can't Be Fixed: Reimagining Counterculture Today*, both published by Melville House. This story is from *The Terrorist's Black Paintings*, a work in progress, in which we discover the discreet charms of domestic terrorism.